BROKEN

CHRISTINE M. MORTON

PAGE PUBLISHING, INC.
Conneaut Lake, PA

First originally published by Page Publishing 2020

ISBN 978-1-6624-0685-0 (pbk)
ISBN 978-1-6624-0686-7 (digital)

Printed in the United States of America

Much, much thanks to my friends and family who supported me throughout this journey. Mom, you were my inspiration to write a book. I wish you were here to read it. Dad, thanks for always being there for me! To my husband Steve, and sons Tyler and Cheyne, I love you and thank you so much for the encouragement, love, and support. Rebecca Rohan, I could not have done this without you!

This book is dedicated to my mom and dad for always believing in me no matter what. I love you both!

CHAPTER I

Chance

"The drink. Oh my god, the drink."

Roughly Half an Hour Earlier

"Please calm down. You're getting yourself all worked up. And over what? Nothing! How many times are we going to go through this? Amanda—do you even hear what I'm saying?" Chance tried to calmly reason with the frantic blue-eyed, black-haired beauty, but Amanda just kept swinging and cursing loudly.

Chance's mind raced, as he wasn't quite sure how to handle the situation. Each time Amanda swung, Chance would use his arms to protect his face and take a step back. He wasn't the type of guy to hit a girl regardless of how angry he became. Unfortunately for him, Amanda didn't think twice about hitting him. When Amanda was upset over something, there was no reasoning with her. All Chance could do was wait as she got it all out of her system. Just like each other time, this one too would pass.

"I saw you with that whore, Chance! Don't try and deny it!" Amanda screamed at the top of her lungs, swinging again at him but missing, punching the air.

"Amanda, that whore you keep screaming at me about is your best friend! I don't understand why you keep accusing me of hitting on her. We attend the same gym, so yes, there are times that I say hi to her, but I do that because she's your best friend! If it was just some random chick, I wouldn't even think twice about saying hi!" Chance said in exasperation. "Honestly, Amanda, I don't know how much more I can handle of this crazy behavior. You're beyond out of control. This is ridiculous." Before Chance could even get another word out, he noticed the glare Amanda was giving him, and it sent chills up and down his spine.

"Are you trying to break up with me?" Amanda asked through gritted teeth. "How dare you threaten me!" As Amanda went to take another swing at him, Chance was able to grab her arm and swing her around so that her back was right up against his chest. He wrapped both of his arms around her and squeezed tightly so that she couldn't escape his hold on her.

With his lips pressing up against her right ear, he calmly whispered his explanation for what she thought she'd perceived. "What you witnessed was Leeza walking into the gym as I was walking out of the gym. We said hi to one another. That's it! Amanda, we've been together for seven years, we're engaged to be married, so why's it we have to go through this silly game over and over again? What's it that I have to do to make you understand that I love only you!" Chance pleaded. "I've been nothing but good to you. I've never given you reason to doubt me, but you do."

The almost straitjacket grip and the feel of Chance's soft lips and hot breath up against her ear started to make Amanda aroused. Chance could feel the tension melting away as she gradually began to relax. While he loosened his grip, her arms dropped to her sides like she was holding on to heavy weights. Amanda gradually turned around to face Chance. She looked him dead in the eye and then dropped to the floor.

CHAPTER 2

Lena

At nineteen years old, I felt as though I was one of the most laid-back, caring teenagers anyone could know. No one ever bothered to get to know me, but they sure didn't think twice about judging me. Most people always looked at me like I was just some prissy, stuck-up blond bitch, but that couldn't have been further from the truth.

My dad, Joe, my mom, Rita, and I lived in a colonial-style home that was set back from the main road, Kelsey Avenue, behind some tall brush. Our house isn't big at all, but it was big enough for the three of us. I had no siblings, at least that I was aware of.

A big red barn sits next to our house that held our three horses, two cows, and ten chickens. Growing up, it was my job to brush the horses, milk the cows, and gather the eggs. The milk and eggs were our main source of food and income back then. Now I work at Frederick's, the local grocery store. In high school, they always asked what you wanted to be when you grew up, and I never had an answer to that. As a matter of fact, I still don't. For the time being, I'll just continue working at Frederick's and see where life takes me.

My mom passed away when I was sixteen. I took it bad. Because I didn't have any siblings, she was first and foremost my mom, but she was also my best friend and confidante. Very few people can say that. My mom fell ill when I was eleven years old. Taking care of her was my main priority, which is in part why I didn't and still don't have many friends. I'm not blaming my mom by any means. It was my choice to take care of her, and I would've done anything for her. She was by far the best mom in the whole world.

Most kids got together and played outside when they got out of school. Not me. While my dad was at work, I'd come straight home to be with and take care of my mom. Each day after school was the same for me. I'd try to get my mom to eat whatever little bit of food she could in an effort to try to keep her strength up for the next round of chemo treatments. When I said my mom was ill, I meant very ill, unfortunately with cancer. Ovarian cancer, also known as the silent killer.

Every night before bed, my mom and I'd watch movies together and then we'd sing and pray together. I'd read her part of a book before we both turned in for the night. Taking care of my mom was like having a full-time job. The sorrow I felt inside was eating away at me, but I still woke up and went about my day with a smile on my face. If my dad wasn't out working hard all day every day, I know he'd have helped my mom in any way that he could, but unfortunately, somebody had to pay the bills.

That was until the dreadful day I came home from school and my dad was on the porch sitting in the white wicker rocking chair, which was a wedding gift from my grandparents, with tears streaming down his face. I'll never forget what he said to me that day, "Lena, honey, the Lord came and took your momma today. It was her time, and now she's up in heaven." I could tell my dad was trying very hard to keep his composure for me.

I remember standing there for a minute or two before dropping my schoolbag and running over to him and just wrapping my arms around him as tightly as I could and letting the tears pour out. I had known that day was coming, but you can never really prepare yourself for the day it actually happens and then someone you love is gone. Forever.

It wasn't until I met him.

At my mother's wake of all places. He helped me pick up the broken pieces of my heart that were currently shattered. He, too, had lost his mom.

Chapter 3

Chance

"Amanda?" Chance said in an unsure, shaky manner. "Amanda, this isn't funny," Chance pressed on in a stern voice. He reached down to touch Amanda, and when she didn't respond, he dropped down on his hands and knees and placed his ear on her chest, listening for signs of a heartbeat. When no sound emanated from her chest, Chance frantically started to pump where her heartbeat should've been and also performed mouth-to-mouth resuscitation in an effort to get her breathing again. Once Chance recognized that she wasn't responding to the CPR efforts, he immediately jumped to his feet, darted for the phone, and as quickly as his shaking hands would allow him, he punched in the numbers 9-1-1.

"Nine, one, one, what's your emergency?" a calm voice asked from the other end of the receiver.

"Hello...she fell...Amanda...she fell. I don't know what happened," Chance stammered.

"Okay, sir, I'm going to need you to calm down. Give me your name, and I need you to tell me what happened," said the calm voice.

"Chance. My name is Chance Wallace. My...my girlfriend...I mean fiancée, she fell, and I don't know what happened."

"Okay, Mr. Wallace, take a couple of deep breaths. Can you tell me where she fell? Was it down a flight of stairs?"

Before the calm voice could continue, Chance, not intentionally, cut her off, "She just passed out right in front of me onto the kitchen floor."

"Okay, that's good, Mr. Wallace. Is she breathing? Does she have a heartbeat?"

"No for both," Chance said through his tears.

"Mr. Wallace, give me your address so we can get somebody out to you right away."

"It's, um. It's, um…78. It's 78 Dupont Street…Oh my god, she's not breathing! Please hurry!" Chance whimpered.

"We're having someone dispatched as we speak. Stay calm."

"I need someone now, right now," the calm voice heard Chance say as his voice trailed off, followed by a loud crash, which was from Chance dropping the phone out of his hand.

Chance lay down next to Amanda's body and put his arm across her chest. His mind was reeling, trying to comprehend what happened, and just as that thought was going through his mind, he sprang into an upright position. "The drink! Oh my god, the drink! No, no, no, no, no this isn't happening," Chance kept repeating to himself as he headed up the stairs toward their bedroom on the second floor.

There it was. Completely empty. Every last drop. Gone. The drinking glass sat there tauntingly, just as he had left it, only now it was empty without the deadly concoction filling it. Chance's mind began to race as he now realized what had occurred. He launched himself into the bathroom, just making it to the toilet before ferociously vomiting into it.

Then the doorbell rang.

CHAPTER 4

Lena

I was sitting in a chair in the corner of the dining room when he approached and introduced himself.

"Hello. My name is Bryan, Bryan Mills," he said, extending his hand out to me.

It turns out we went to school together. Me having no knowledge that we were in some of the same classes goes to show just how out of it I'd been while taking care of my mother.

"I'm Lena. Nice to meet you," I said, returning the handshake. This small gesture brought a smile to my face, but this just wasn't the place or time to be happy, so my smile quickly faded.

"Do you mind if I take a seat?" he asked kindly.

My body stiffened up some as I tried to figure out why this handsome, blue-eyed, blond stranger wanted to interact with me.

Then he began to tell me his story, and that's when I learned that we had something in common.

"I somewhat know how you're feeling. My mom passed away when I was eight. Then my dad walked out on me and left me alone to fend for myself as soon as I turned sixteen." Bryan looked down at his hands, which were clasped, but his thumbs moved rapidly in a circular motion.

"Luckily for me," he continued, "my grandparents had paid the house off as an anniversary gift to my parents, so I don't have to worry about paying a mortgage. I just have to pay the utility bills."

"That's terrible! Aren't you lonely?" I inquired, feeling bitter toward his father, whom I've never met.

"No, not at all," he said, shaking his head back and forth. "I feel relieved more than anything. My dad was an alcoholic. He wasn't always an alcoholic, though. It happened after my mom died. I'd come home from school every day to find him passed out in different areas of the house. Living with an alcoholic is basically like living alone, so I became acclimated to that lifestyle. I taught myself how to cook, clean, do laundry, and even drive."

Bryan went on to tell me how he didn't have any friends. He said he was always too shy to talk to anyone, so he always just kept to himself. He said he saw me all the time and knew we lived close by one another, but he said I wore a bitch face most of the time, and I always looked so serious that he was afraid to approach me. That bitch face, of course, was me trying hard not to cry at school knowing my mom was at home dying.

I would have never guessed in a million years that me and the cute, blue-eyed, blond boy up the road would become so close. Sometimes too close. Sometimes for the good and sometimes for the bad.

If I knew then what I know now, maybe things wouldn't have happened the way they did.

CHAPTER 5

Chance

Chance could hear his heart pulsating fast in his ears. His stare that was fixated on the empty glass was broken by the sound of the doorbell ringing.

"Police! Open up!" Chance heard them yelling. Unsure what to do next, he hurriedly darted down the stairs, toward the front door to greet the police officers, leaving the empty glass sitting on the end table.

———

Prior to Amanda arriving home, Chance had already known what he was in for. This wouldn't be the first time, nor would it be the last time, they would argue over this. He didn't really know much about bipolar disorder, except for the crazy ups and downs of emotions he experienced weekly with his soon-to-be wife, Amanda Keele. While saying hi to Leeza outside of the gym entrance, Chance had spotted Amanda's red Kia Sportage speeding by.

Seriously? You must be kidding me, Chance thought to himself. As he sat in his truck, Chance contemplated what his next move was going to be. Heading home, panic-driven, he considered just driving his truck full speed straight into a tree. That was until he realized that there was a possibility of him surviving the crash and becoming crippled for the rest of his life. The thought of that happening made him cringe. As that thought passed, another thought popped into his mind. "That'll be perfect," he said out loud, but to himself.

When Chance turned to pull into the driveway, he noticed that the red Kia Sportage wasn't there yet. *Odd*, Chance thought. He kicked himself into high gear as he raced into the house, knowing she could pull in any second. On his way into the house, he whispered to himself the ingredients as he grabbed them: from the garage, "antifreeze"; then through the kitchen, "small glass"; into the dining room, "whiskey"; up the stairs, through the bedroom into the final destination, the bathroom.

Chance grabbed pills randomly from the medicine cabinet, medicine that helped treat Amanda's bipolar disorder and pain meds that he'd saved for no good reason from a surgery he'd had to have on his left hand. Using the bottom of the glass, Chance crushed all the pills until they were just a white pile of dust. He cupped his right hand and slid the white powder off the bathroom counter and into the glass, then he proceeded to pour the antifreeze in. Lastly, he poured in some whiskey, then added a splash of water to top it off.

Chance took the glass, full of the deadly concoction, and placed it on the end table next to the bed, closest to the bathroom, where he intended to chug it.

First, even though he knew Amanda could walk in at any moment, Chance couldn't fathom the thought of his body being found smelly and unclean, so he fleetingly jumped in the shower.

The moment Chance placed one foot out of the shower, he heard the front door slam.

"Where are you, you stupid, cheating son of a bitch?" Amanda screamed from the lower floor. Chance snatched the first shirt and pair of shorts he could unearth in their messy bedroom and, as he ran down the stairs, asked her in a low, sturdy, voice to "please calm down."

————

"Hello, Officers, thank God you're here," Chance said, panting, and though winded, he managed to say, "My fiancée…she's…over… there," pointing to Amanda's lifeless body lying on the kitchen floor.

"Please help her. Please. Please help her. Please help…"

Chapter 6

Lena

"It was a pleasure to meet you, Lena. I know the circumstances are shitty, but you should stop by sometime. I'm literally right up the dirt road." Bryan laughed, looking down at his feet. When I responded with "Sure," Bryan's head flew up so quickly he almost lost his balance. "Really?" he unintentionally shouted. Then he tried to cover up his astonishment by changing his voice a bit, "I mean, wow, that's great. I look forward to us hanging out." Then he casually turned and walked out our front door.

From that day on, Bryan and I were inseparable. We would take turns at one another's house, eating, playing board games, playing card games, watching movies, and occasionally having sleepovers. However, the sleepovers mostly took place at my house, and my dad was sure to separate the two of us, making Bryan sleep on the couch in the living room. Sometimes all three of us would fall asleep in the living room while watching a movie. We were what I liked to call the Three Stooges. Bryan spent pretty much every holiday with us, seeing as he didn't have any family in town to celebrate with. My dad didn't mind. He really liked Bryan.

Dressed in his tight blue jeans, flannel button-up shirt, cowboy boots, and hat, Bryan took his morning stroll, like he did every day. To my house.

"Morning, li'l lady," he said, tipping his hat. "Let's see, it is 7:45 a.m., and your shift starts in twenty-five minutes. I suggest you hurry on up so we both aren't late for work."

Of course, when I'm rushed, I tend to get nervous and more forgetful. Who am I kidding—it's like this every morning. "Keys, check. Name tag, check. Purse, check. Phone, oh no, where's my phone, where's my phone, where's my—okay, got it! Let's go," I said breathlessly as I ran past Bryan and through the front door. Then I stopped, turned around, and gave Bryan a peck on his cheek. "Morning," I said, grinning.

Together, we walked down Webster Lane, the dirt path that we called home, and then onto the main strip of Kelsey Avenue. First, we stopped at Frederick's, and then Bryan would continue the stroll alone to his job at the local factory, Constantine's, which was literally across the way. This became a normal routine for us.

I usually prepared our lunches the night before. Then on the way to our jobs, we'd talk about the latest news or what we thought might happen that day at work. Honestly, nothing big happened here in the small town of Silver Tree Acres.

At least nothing used to.

On rainy days, Bryan would pick me up in his shiny '92 blue Chevy pickup, his baby, that he bought with his own hard-earned money.

After each our shifts ended, at 5:00 p.m., Bryan would meet me back at Frederick's, and then we'd walk or drive home and discuss what was going to be on the menu for dinner that evening. Lame, I know! Sometimes my dad would surprise us and have dinner already cooked, but that didn't happen quite as frequently as it used to.

———

"I think today we should have pork chops with mashed potatoes and applesauce! Yum!" I screamed, bouncing up and down like a little kid in a candy store. Bryan gave me a funny look, where his one eyebrow went way up and the other one went way down, pretty much looking at me like I was crazy, before he agreed. "That does sound really good! Should we eat at my place or yours?"

"Well, seeing as my dad called me at work and said he had something really important to talk to us about, I'm going to say my place!"

"Your place it is!"

I wonder what's so important, I thought to myself.

When Bryan and I arrived at my house, I let Bryan know that I was going to quickly change into something more comfortable before meeting him in the kitchen.

I was wearing my old, worn-out Mickey Mouse sweatshirt and red sweatpants with my bright-pink fuzzy slippers when I greeted Bryan in the kitchen.

"Sexy," Bryan said in a mysteriously deep voice. I shot him my "are you serious" look that must've had "shut up, jerk" written all over it.

"Sorry…I meant, my, how beautiful you look!" Bryan tried again, smiling.

"Ha-ha, very funny, smart-ass! Can we please concentrate on cooking now and not on my wardrobe? When I passed my dad on the way to the kitchen, he looked awfully upset." *I really hope he's not going to tell us he has a terminal illness. I don't know if I can handle anything like that again.* Then I stopped for a moment to gather my thoughts as I realized I was jumping to conclusions.

"Potatoes are cut!" Bryan sang loudly.

"You're such a goofball," I tried to say while laughing.

I grabbed the eggs, raw pork chops, and seasoned breadcrumbs and worked my magic to give them my special touch. Bryan turned the oven on to preheat before putting the water for the potatoes on the stove. After I spread the pork chops out on the cookie sheet, preparing them to go into the oven, I started chopping up the salad, tomatoes, and cucumbers as a side dish. Once the potatoes were on the stove and pork chops in the oven, Bryan and I sat down at the kitchen table to have a glass of wine.

Bryan and I started to debate over what the movie of the night was going to be when my dad walked into the kitchen, startling us.

My dad took a deep breath, holding his beer in his right hand, and as he exhaled, he said, "Listen up, guys, I have to tell you something."

CHAPTER 7

Chance

Amanda slammed the front door as hard as she possibly could in an effort to get Chance's attention. When Chance didn't respond, she thought to herself, *He had to have heard me slam the door. How could he not?* She waited a couple more minutes before deciding to greet him instead.

As Amanda headed up the stairs toward their bedroom, she could hear the shower running. "No wonder he didn't come running," she griped to herself under her breath. Then her mind began to wander.

That son of a bitch is taking a shower because he's trying to cover something up! Amanda convinced herself. Her blood began to boil at the thought of her fiancé and best friend hooking up behind her back. She wholeheartedly believed that Chance and Leeza had slept together. *Even if Leeza just gave him a blow job, he'd have to wash the lipstick off his dick,* she thought. *Ugh! this is so frustrating,* Amanda whimpered to herself, feeling sick to her stomach at the thought of it.

Finally reaching the bedroom, unsure how to approach the situation at hand, Amanda noticed a glass with alcohol sitting next to the bed. Curious as to what was in the glass, Amanda quickly ran over to take a whiff of the liquid. "Whiskey? Ha! I'll show that fucker," she mumbled to herself as she tipped the glass back and swallowed the greenish-brown liquid in one gulp. She figured this wouldn't only piss him off but would help calm her nerves as well so that she would have enough courage to confront him about his cheating ways.

The shower turned off, and Amanda decided at the last minute to run back downstairs to try the slamming door technique again, hoping this time he'd hear it and come running to her like the little bitch he was. She tiptoed down the stairs back into the kitchen, grabbing the knob on the door as gently as she could as to not make any sound. When she successfully opened the door, she had a huge grin on her face.

Quickly and with as much force as she could muster up, she slammed the kitchen door. Immediately, she began ranting and raving like a madwoman, and sure enough, here came Chance running toward her, just as she planned.

CHAPTER 8

Lena

"I've been doing a lot of thinking lately," my dad began, looking directly at Bryan and me.

"Lena, now that your mom is gone and you're all grown up, I don't really have much else left to do here. Please don't take this the wrong way, as if I'm abandoning you, but I feel as though it's time for me to move on. With my own life, that is." Joe paused, looking for some response from us before continuing.

"I've been thinking about purchasing a condo down in Florida… to move there. I've been a countryman all my life, and I know I probably don't have too many years left to live, but I'd like to try and live those years living elsewhere. Somewhere new that I've never been before. Florida seems like a good place to start," Joe said, searching for his daughter's approval.

"In a condo, I won't have to worry about mowing the lawn, or any maintenance work for that matter. It would be all done for me. Plus, it'd give you and even Bryan here a place to go and visit rather than just staying here." Joe paused for a moment before continuing, "I know I'm just breaking this to both of you now, but I'm looking to actually move within the next two weeks."

"Two weeks, seriously?" I yelled out. "Dad—"

"Lena, before you say anything, I just want to let you know this house is paid for, so you do not have to worry about mortgage payments. And hey, you never know, maybe Bryan could even move in here. I mean, he practically lives here anyways." Joe smirked sheepishly at the two of them. "I love you so much, sweetie, but it really is time for Daddy to move on with his life. Maybe you and Bryan could—"

I stopped my dad before he could say another word. "We get the point, Dad," I said, sounding a little bit angrier than I meant to.

Silence filled the room as the three of us just sat there and stared at our drinks on the kitchen table. As I was pulling the pork chops from the oven, I overheard Bryan whisper to my dad, "Give her some time to let it sink in, Mr. McAnderson, and I'm sure she'll come around." Bryan stood up from his chair and nonchalantly went over to prepare the mashed potatoes and help set out the plates. The three of us sat quietly, not speaking one word during dinner. It was definitely awkward.

Bryan broke the silence by offering to clean up after dinner. With my head tilted down toward the kitchen table, I nodded in agreement to Bryan's offer. While Bryan was clearing the table, I looked up at my dad, then stood up and walked out the back door into the yard. Apparently, my dad retreated to the front room.

Bryan stood in the middle of the kitchen, running his hands through his hair, not knowing what to do. He knew how close my dad and I were. It was killing him to know that I was hurt, but he also understood why my father wanted to do it. It was nothing like when his alcoholic father decided to get up and walk out on him, not giving him a warning. This situation was much different, and it caused Bryan a great deal of stress, which he didn't know how to handle.

Later, I wondered if this partly contributed to the decisions he chose to make down the road.

CHAPTER 9

Chance

"Mr. Wallace, can you hear me? Try and open your eyes," echoed a male's voice. "That's it," the voice said, fading in and out as Chance felt a cold compression upon his forehead. Slowly Chance tried to open his eyes, but his eyelids felt heavy, as though they were made of metal. His vision was so blurry all he could make out was a shadow figure and very bright lights. "You hit your head pretty hard, Mr. Wallace. You've a nice goose egg the size of a golf ball on the back of your head," the shadow figure said faintly. "Don't worry, though, we'll take very good care of you."

Black, then silence.

———

"You've a visitor, Mr. Wallace. Would you like me to let her in?" he heard a female voice whisper in his ear.

"Amanda?" Chance asked, springing upright in the hospital bed.

"Be careful, Mr. Wallace, you could have really hurt yourself. Just take it easy."

Chance stared at the figure in front of him then asked through jumbled confusion, "Who're you? Where am I? Is this a hospital? What's going on?" Just as the nurse was about to answer all his questions, his visitor walked in the door.

"Leeza? What's going on? Why am I in a hospital?" As reality started to set in, Chance asked with panic in his voice, "Oh my god, where's Amanda? Is she here with me?"

"Hey, buddy, looking a little on the rough side there," she joked. "Ugh, where are my manners?" Leeza scolded herself. Chance, unfazed by her comments, just sat there, gazing at her and waiting for an answer to his question.

"I came here as fast as I could the moment I heard on the news what happened." As Leeza continued about how sorry she was, Chance thought to himself, *News? News about?* Then it hit him like a ton of bricks.

"It wasn't my fault—" Chance blurted out before Leeza cut him off unintentionally.

"I can't believe Amanda of all people would take her own life. I mean, I feel like I didn't really know her at all. I don't understand what'd make her do such a thing."

"She didn't take her own life—"

But before Chance was able to finish his sentence, Leeza gasped and her hands flew to her mouth in horror. "You k-k-killed her?"

"No!" Chance shouted, startling Leeza and catching the attention of the nurse walking past his room.

"Everything okay in here?" the nurse asked, peeping her head in.

"Yes, we're fine," Chance said apologetically. "I'm sorry, Leeza, I didn't mean to shout and scare you." Chance put his head in his hands. "It's not what you think. It was my fault, but not intentionally by any means whatsoever. Leeza, you know I'd never hurt Amanda. She may've been a crazy, controlling bitch sometimes, but I still loved her," Chance said, tearing up.

"Okay, Chance, I apologize for jumping to conclusions. So what exactly happened to her?" Leeza asked, not quite sure if she wanted to hear the truth, if it was the truth.

Chapter 10

Lena

I really don't know why it bothered me as much as it did about my dad leaving. Fear? It had to be the fear of being alone and growing up, becoming a responsible adult. I felt like I was in a daze while I cashed people out at Frederick's. I'd never really thought about living on my own before, so far away from my dad, the only family I had left. I mean, I knew eventually one day I might've moved out, but I definitely didn't think it'd be this soon, and I certainly didn't think it'd be my dad moving out on me!

"Dear, you rang the sauce up twice," I heard a low-pitched voice say, breaking my trance-like state.

"I'm so sorry, Mrs. Adamski."

Mrs. Adamski was a sweet lady who lived only around the corner from the store. Sometimes she'd come in, and you couldn't get her to stop talking, and then other times she didn't say a word.

"I apologize. Apparently my mind is elsewhere. Let me fix that for you," I said with a forced smile. I couldn't wait until five o'clock rolled around. Today felt like one of the longest days of my life.

———

Once the clock finally hit five on the dot, I took off my apron and made a dash for the front door. The moment I walked out the front doors of Frederick's, Bryan greeted me with a loud "Hello, beautiful!" with his hands in the air. He could tell immediately by the look on my face that I wasn't in the mood.

"You know, Lena, this could be a really good opportunity for your dad. He really doesn't have much left here to do now that his little girl is all grown up. Hey, and maybe like your father said, I could move in with you, if you wanted me to."

I must've shot Bryan a dirty look because he was instantly apologizing and backing away from me with his hands in the air as though he just got caught in a bad act. "Sorry, it was just a thought," he said with his head down and sadness in his voice.

"I know I shouldn't be upset. It's more the fear of not seeing him or hearing his voice every day. I'm not mad at him for wanting to be happy. I'm just going to really miss him. I'll talk to him when I get home so that he doesn't think I'm resentful about his decision."

"That's a great idea," Bryan instantaneously agreed with me. "Hey, it's okay to feel the way you're feeling. You and your father are very close. It's completely natural for you to be upset. If you'd like, I can come with you to talk to him."

"No, I need to do this alone. No offense, but I'd like to spend the evening only with my dad tonight," I said in an apologetic tone.

"Hey, whoa, no, of course!" Bryan stumbled upon his words. "I get it! No worries here from this guy," he said, pointing at himself. "If you need to talk, you know where to find me!"

We were only five minutes away from my house when the rain began to come down in buckets. Bryan and I looked at each other and instantly knew we had the same idea in mind: run!

We held hands as we ran through the rain, and as we turned onto Webster Lane, I purposely pointed to the right. When Bryan turned his head to see what I was pointing at, I let go of his hand and started to run faster, laughing hysterically. I yelled at the top of my lungs, "I'm going to beat you!" smiling back at him. Bryan, not so impressed with my joke, began to try and catch up with me, yelling, "That was so unfair!"

Bryan and I were completely drenched by the time we stepped onto my porch. As we were trying to catch our breath, our eyes locked. There was something about seeing Bryan completely wet. He looked different. He looked...sexy.

From his stare, he might've been thinking the same thing about me.

We both took a step forward, our faces slowly inching toward each other. Just as my lips brushed up against his, a crack of thunder shook the ground, startling us to the point we both practically jumped out of our skin.

Bryan and I looked at each other and were in hysterics like two little kids who'd just heard someone say the word *fart* for the very first time.

"Okay then," I said, swinging one foot over the other and turning toward my front door. "I think that may've been a sign that I should be going now."

"Good luck with your dad tonight. You got this!" Bryan cheered, putting a fist in the air. "If it's still raining tomorrow, I'll pick you up in the truck. Good night, Lena." He bent over, making a silly hand gesture as if he were bidding farewell to the Queen of England. Then off Bryan ran in the pouring rain, in the direction of his house.

CHAPTER 11

Chance

Chance took a deep breath. "Leeza, this is what I think happened, and the intention was to hurt myself, not Amanda, I swear," Chance spoke softly as he looked down at the white medical bedsheet that covered the bottom half of his body, trying to avoid eye contact with Leeza.

"I made a nasty mixture, a deadly mixture, of antifreeze, pain meds, and some of Amanda's medicine she took for her bipolar disorder. I made the mixture, and then stupid me decided it'd be a good idea to be clean prior to dying, so I hopped in the shower, leaving the—"

"Stop, stop, stop right there!" Leeza interrupted. "The cops think it was a suicide. It's all over the news right now." Leeza reached for the television remote.

"No! Please don't turn that on. I don't want to hear about whatever crazy story they have tossed together for the drama-hungry public," Chance declared, sounding defeated. He covered his face with his hands, and as he dragged his hands down the front of his face, he mumbled in a whimper, "Leeza, what am I going to do?"

Leeza reached over and removed Chance's hands from his face, looked him dead in the eyes, and said, "You mean to say what you're *not* going to do!"

Chance looked at Leeza quizzically.

"Chance, Amanda was my best friend. I know how crazy your relationship was with her. She wasn't an easy person to date, or even understand for that matter. I know she not only mentally abused you,

28

she sometimes physically abused you too. And you took it and you dealt with it! No man or woman should ever have to deal with what you went through. I know you didn't know any other way because she was your one and only high school sweetheart, but this is your chance at a new beginning! Move someplace far away from here. Start your life over. Amanda was all you ever knew. Go out and explore the world. Live life at its best. You need time to heal and think things through. Imagine all the things you could do without someone constantly watching over your shoulder, spying on you, and controlling your every move. I know you loved Amanda, I don't doubt that one bit, but the coast is clear. Get out of town now while you can. Go find your true soul mate. She's still waiting out there. Go find her."

Chance was silent for a couple seconds. He wasn't sure if Leeza was serious or joking, but by the expression on her face, he believed she was serious.

"Thank you, Leeza," Chance said, taking her hand in his. "I appreciate the kind words and advice. I'm really going to take what you said into consideration."

"Chance, I mean you need to go, like, right now while you still can. What you and I know about the situation will be our little secret, but leave now in case they put the pieces together, if they ever do. Don't risk the possibility of going to prison for the rest of your life."

"But it was an accident!" Chance cried.

"That's not how the cops are going to see it," Leeza said matter-of-factly.

———

At the sound of the alarm bell, four nurses ran to room 104 to check on the patient, who, from the sounds of it, had flatlined. Upon entering the room, they found the bed in a jumbled mess, sheets on the floor, drops of blood from the IVs that were at one point inserted into Chance's left arm, and an open window next to the bed.

Chance had nothing but the clothes he had worn to the hospital. He had no idea where he was going or what he was going to do, but one thing was for sure, today was the first day of the new chapter of his life. Chance smiled at the thought as he walked toward the train station booth to buy his one-way ticket out of town.

CHAPTER 12

Lena

Wow, what the heck just happened? I grinned to myself. When I walked in the front door, I was greeted with the smell of garlic mixed with simmering sauce and pasta. This made my stomach growl. I guess that short run home worked off whatever bit of lunch I had left in my stomach.

"Lena, you're soaked!" my dad said, startling me. "I'm sorry, sweetie, I didn't mean to scare you. Go clean up and change into some dry clothes and meet me back down in the kitchen. Dinner's ready!" He sounded so proud of himself.

I ran upstairs and within five minutes was back down in my favorite outfit, sweatpants, and a T-shirt. I confidently walked into the kitchen, where my dad was smiling ear to ear as he dished out our food.

"Dad, I just want to apologize for the way I acted yesterday. I guess I was just—" I didn't get to finish my sentence as my dad interrupted me with a stern, "Shhh."

"Lena, let's just enjoy this meal together, then we can speak our minds. Does that sound fair?"

"Fair enough," I replied.

Quietly we enjoyed our spaghetti dinner at the kitchen table with a glass of our favorite wine. Suddenly an unexpected crack of thunder, so loud it shook the house, made me and my dad both jump practically out of our seats, leaving us in stitches.

Once we finished eating, I gathered all the dishes from the table and stove and washed them while my dad dried and put them away.

This father-daughter moment brought tears to my eyes, as I reminisced about the past and about the future when my dad would no longer be here to complete this small task with me anymore.

After the dishes were done, Dad and I went into the family room, where he sat in his favorite chocolate-brown leather chair and I plopped my stuffed self on the opposite end of the light suede sofa.

"Dinner was great, Dad. Thanks for cooking. Listen, I was being selfish yesterday when you told me you wanted to move to Florida. I'm sorry. I'm really happy for you. I think this move is going to be great for you. I guess I have to learn to grow up some time," I said through sniffles and laughter.

I could see tears brimming in my dad's eyes when he replied, "Thank you. I feel this move would be in the best interest for the both of us. You need to live your own life and not be bothered with having to take care of your old man. As a matter of fact, you should have a man of your own to start taking care of you! Then I can come back to visit for the wedding…hint, hint. Or if you would rather have a destination wedding, you can come to Florida and get married on the beach," my dad said, smiling and winking.

"Um, Dad, I hate to burst your bubble, but in order to get married, you kind of need to have a fiancé, and in order to have a fiancé, you kind of need to have a boyfriend, which if you remember I don't have either," I said sarcastically.

My dad got up from his chair, sat next to me on the couch, put his arms around me, and said, "Let's have a movie night, just the two of us!"

"Can I pick the movie?" I asked excitedly.

"Absolutely!"

It looked as though my dad was going to say something else, but then *Pet Cemetery* started to play on the television.

CHAPTER 13

Chance

Chance looked out the train window at the beautiful foliage, but instead of taking in the beautiful scenery, he kept thinking about everything that had happened with Amanda. He wondered why he really didn't feel very sad or upset. Instead, he felt relieved. Free.

The train was at the last stop before it was to head back to Cloverfield, Maine. Chance stepped off the train and read the sign out loud, but in a low enough voice that only he could hear, "Silver Tree Acres, Pennsylvania. This is home now."

It was late. Chance was still in his hospital gown, with his jacket on and his wallet with only a couple hundred dollars in it. *First things first*, he thought, *find somewhere to sleep!* While looking for a hotel, Chance saw a Walmart sign in the distance. *Clothes would definitely be good before walking into a hotel,* he thought to himself. People were gawking at him as he exited the train station, and he knew it was because of his outfit.

Chance carried the items he bought into the Walmart bathroom to change. He threw the hospital gown in the garbage and walked out feeling like a new man.

On his way out of Walmart was the first time he noticed the blond-haired, blue-eyed beauty.

"Excuse you," a tall, heavyset gentleman said as Chance bounced off his belly.

"Sorry, I'm so—" Chance began.

"Just watch where you're going!" the angry voice said, trailing away.

When Chance looked back, the beauty was gone. He thought about going back in to find her, but then realized just how tired he was and thought it best to go find somewhere to sleep.

Down a couple of blocks from the Walmart was a Hilton, but Chance knew with the amount of cash he had on him, he could not afford a Hilton. Luckily across the street was a motel with the bright-red sign flashing "Vacancy." *Bingo!*

While Chance was checking into the motel, he peered through the window behind the clerk and noticed a little hole-in-the-wall called Mandy's. As soon as Chance got the key and checked out his room, he decided to wander over to Mandy's for a late-night drink.

Chance took a seat at the bar and ordered his favorite, a Jack and Coke. He took a sip of the drink, then thought, *What the hell, no one knows me around here, and I've absolutely nowhere to be tomorrow,* threw the drink back like it was a shot rather than an eight-ounce glass, then ordered another round.

Chance could hear laughter to his left, and when he peered back, he saw a group of girls whispering and giggling to one another, looking right in his direction. *No!* Chance thought to himself. *Too soon.*

A half hour passed, and the girl chatter quieted down. While Chance sat watching the flat-screen TV at the bar, he felt hot breath on the back of his neck and heard a woman's voice whispering in his ear, "Wanna get laid, big boy?"

He thought about it for a moment. *No, Chance,* he heard his inner voice saying to him, *we don't pick up strange girls and have sex with them.* He was about to turn the girl down, but when he turned around, all he could see were large, perky, perfectly round breasts in his face. Chance and Amanda had not had sex in over two months. That was his punishment when Amanda was mad at him. Seeing those breasts and realizing he hadn't had sex in over two months, Chance didn't mean to, but he couldn't help getting an erection, which was visibly noticeable to the large-breasted redhead, and she took that as a yes to her question.

Chance couldn't keep his hands off the redheaded stranger's breasts and at the same time was imagining the hot blonde he saw earlier at Walmart. He squeezed her breasts over and over, and the angrier he got over the thought of the Amanda situation, he pounded himself so hard into her he didn't hear her cries for him to stop. Before he knew it, it was over. He couldn't hold it any longer. Her soft, wet insides felt so good he came as hard as he could right into her.

Afterward, he plopped down on the bed and fell fast asleep.

When he awoke the next morning, she was gone. No name, no note, no goodbye.

CHAPTER 14

Lena

"Any plans for the long weekend coming up?" Margie inquired.

Margie was such a sweet lady. Her shoulder-length hair was as white as snow, and even with white hair, she was a very attractive woman, especially for being in her early sixties. Margie wore her hair up all the time at work. The only time I'd see her hair down was when I ran into her at the local bar, Peeves, with her man, Sam, whom she claims was not her man or boyfriend, even though they slept together practically every night. And when I say sleep, I mean have sex! She referred to Sam as her boy toy. And yes, she was a frequent flyer at the bar. She could actually outdrink me! Margie had been like a mother hen to me since my mom had passed away. She took me under her wing as if I was one of her own. All her children were grown up and had moved out of state.

"Bryan and I were thinking of renting a cabin at Sundown Valley for a couple of days," I replied to Margie's question.

"You know, you and that Bryan Mills spend an awful lot of time together. You two would make a good couple," Margie chuckled.

"Whoa, whoa, Margie! Let's not go there. Bryan and I are just friends," I said with my hands up in the air.

"Friends that do everything *together*!" Margie said with a sly smile on her face. I could only imagine what that little old lady brain was thinking in there.

———

As five o'clock rolled around, Bryan was standing in his usual spot outside of Frederick's waiting for me.

"He's kind of cute, all hot, sweaty, and dirty," Margie said, nudging me in my side.

"Now, now, Margie, wipe the drool from the side of your mouth," I joked.

"Go get him, tiger," Margie growled as she gave me a small shove out the front door. When I looked back at her to give her the "you are too crazy" face, she was making a cat-clawing motion with her hands. *She's too much*, I thought, giggling to myself.

"Should I ask why Margie was pushing you through the front door and clawing at you?" Bryan asked with one eyebrow lifted.

"No!" I shouted unintentionally.

"Yikes. Okay, okay," Bryan said, holding his hands up in surrender. "So did you hear about the redhead they found in a field not too far from here? The news said she was mangled up pretty bad."

"No, I did not. If you forgot, I was working all day, unlike some people apparently," I quipped.

"There was a ton of blood!" Bryan began.

"Can we not talk about that, Debbie Downer? It's kind of creeping me out!" I instantly spoiled Bryan's excitement.

"Okay. Sorry. So anyways, how was your day?"

"It was okay. Margie was asking what the big plans were for the upcoming long weekend, so I told her about our camping trip, and she got all weird on me."

"Weird like how?"

"She kept making silly comments on how close you and I are. That's when you witnessed her making that strange clawing gesture with her hands. Don't worry, though, I kept reassuring her there is nothing going on between us, that we're just friends!"

"Why would I worry?" Bryan asked, his voice a little lower.

"Well, 'cause, you know, you are like my big brother."

"Ouch!" he said, making a stabbing motion toward his heart. "Really? Big brother? Lena, please tell me you are joking. We almost kissed the other day, so are you saying you would make out with your own brother if you had one?"

"Ew, no! I love our friendship. I don't want you getting all weird on me. That's why I decided to walk away and not go through with it." I looked over at Bryan and with a bit of hesitation in my voice asked, "Well, I would imagine that you think of me kind of like your little sister, right?"

"Sure. Whatever you say, li'l sis," he replied, punching me gently in my arm.

I could tell by Bryan's voice he was being sarcastic. The rest of the walk home was awkwardly quiet. I began to wonder if I might have offended him with my comments. He kept his head down, like he was interested in his feet, the rest of the walk home. He didn't even walk me up to my porch like he always did.

Instead, he turned toward me, gave me a quick hug, and rushed off.

CHAPTER 15

Chance

"What happened to me last night? One minute there were boobs, red hair, sex, then nothing. Black. That's all I can remember," Chance said to his reflection in the mirror. He looked down and noticed that there was dirt underneath his fingernails. *Huh,* he thought to himself. *That's strange.*

Without a second thought about the dirt under his fingernails, Chance hopped into the shower. With his eyes closed and the water spraying his face, he kept seeing flashbacks of the night before. Her breath on his neck, the stumble-walk back to the motel, not so much the taking off the clothes, but the naked bodies, *And damn was her body banging,* the slippery wetness of her pussy. Chance became real hard at the thought and felt that he had no option but to give himself a hand job to feel release. *I am loving this new start of my life,* he thought to himself.

Chance's goal for the day was to start looking for a job. After getting dressed, he headed over to a nearby diner, grabbing a local newspaper on the way. Chance slipped into a booth and ordered coffee and the Big Slam, which consisted of scrambled eggs, bacon, hash browns, and toast, which had to be very lightly toasted or he wouldn't eat it. While Chance waited for his food to come, he began flipping through the paper, looking for the employment section, when something else caught his eye.

"Cassandra Downing, 51, mother of 3, found mutilated in a ditch that runs along Route 5." When Chance looked to the left-hand side of the article, there was the large-breasted redhead staring back at him. Chance dropped the newspaper suddenly and raised his hands up to his mouth as he felt the vomit rise in his throat. He ran toward the bathroom, where he projectile vomited into the toilet.

What the fuck? What the fuck happened last night? Chance's mind was racing. He didn't understand why he could not remember anything after he and the redhead had sex. Then he thought about the dirt under his fingernails this morning. He closed his eyes and shook his head, *No, no, no, no, no,* like he was trying to convince himself that this was all a bad dream. Unfortunately, as fate would have it, he wasn't dreaming.

Chance walked out of the bathroom feeling like all eyes were on him, like everyone knew something he didn't, like he was guilty of a crime he didn't even know he committed. He walked right past the table where his coffee and breakfast plate sat steaming, slung a twenty on the table, and continued walking right out of the front door.

Chance walked right back to his motel room, slammed the door shut, sat on the edge of the bed, put his head in his hands, and began to weep, straining to try to put the pieces of last night back together. *What have I done?*

CHAPTER 16

Lena

My dad was sitting on the porch reading an old war novel when I got home. He looked up and must have noticed that I was stressed. I was sure it was written all over my face.

"Is everything okay, Lena? Where's Bryan?"

"I think he may be upset with me," I mumbled. "I'm not really sure why, though. We were walking, having a great conversation. I told him about what Margie was joking with me about at work, then suddenly his mood changed. He became very quiet."

"Well, what was Margie joking about?" my dad persisted.

"Margie said Bryan and I were very close, and I told Bryan not to worry, that I told Margie that he was like my big brother."

"Oh, no, you didn't, did you?" my dad asked, cringing. "You probably broke that poor guy's heart." My dad looked at me and in the sincerest voice said, "Lena, most men do not like to hear the words 'I love you like a brother.' It is equivalent to a punch in the face for a guy."

"But Bryan is like a big brother to me," I replied, confused.

"I understand, but next time you may want to keep it to yourself and not say it out loud. Just a little fatherly advice," my dad said, smiling.

"I will keep that in mind next time! On another note, Dad, did you pack your things?"

"No, I was waiting for you to get home so that we could pack together." With that said, my dad and I headed into the house to start cooking dinner and packing his things for the move that was coming up very quickly. Bryan and I were to drop my dad off at the airport prior to heading to Sundown Valley for the weekend.

My dad and I whipped up some fish sticks and mac and cheese for dinner. We quickly ate our meal at the dining room table. Afterward, I washed the dishes as my dad headed upstairs to start packing.

We packed until 11:00 p.m., then finally gave in, put our night-clothes on, popped some popcorn, and sat on the couch in the living room to watch the eleven-o'clock news. The top story happened to be about the murdered redhead Bryan had spoken about earlier.

"Wow, it has been years since there has been a murder on this side of town," my dad said. "That is a little too close to home for me! Maybe I should stay here and not move to Florida."

"Dad, seriously! I will be fine! I can handle myself, plus I'll have Bryan to watch over me," I said with a little giggle.

"I don't know about that, honey. After today, he may want nothing more to do with you!" My dad and I looked at each other and started laughing hysterically.

———

I woke up the next morning with the sun shining bright in my eyes. I already had a feeling today was going to be a good day. Bryan and I had made plans earlier in the week to go to Peeves for a couple of drinks after work.

As I walked down the stairs, I noticed Bryan conversing with my dad. This put a big smile on my face. My dad's face seemed to light up too when he saw me approaching them.

"Good mornin', li'l lady, you look like a big ray of sunshine!" Bryan said as he tipped his cowboy hat. "Your dad and I were just talking about the big move tomorrow. Are you ready for that?"

"As ready as I can be, I guess," I replied with sadness in my voice.

"She's a big girl. She can handle it," my dad chimed in, winking at me.

As Bryan and I were about to walk out the front door, I turned to my dad to remind him, "Dad, don't forget, Bryan and I are going for drinks after work tonight. Don't wait up for us."

"Aye, aye, captain," my dad said, saluting me. "On your way now, kiddies, don't want to be late for work!"

Bryan and I made our way down the porch steps, down the winding dirt road, and started on our way toward our jobs, to begin, as what I said earlier, the start of a good day.

CHAPTER 17

Chance

Chance sat at the edge of the bed, running everything through his mind about the night before. *There is no way I could have killed that woman and not remember one single thing about the murder, is there? One, what would I have used as a murder weapon?* He didn't own a gun or a knife—heck, he didn't even have any plastic silverware. *Two, wouldn't there be blood everywhere? Three, how would I have gotten her body from here to Route 5?*

Chance was convinced he did not commit this crime. Instead of wasting the day away worrying about how the redhead had ended up in a ditch over by Route 5, he pulled himself together, grabbed his wallet, and went out the door. He needed a car, and he needed to find a job.

There was not much of a selection to choose from at the used-car dealership, at least that he could afford. He ended up picking out an old, rusty, rundown orange 1994 sedan. And even though it was old and rundown, Chance didn't have enough cash to pay for the total amount and had to make payment arrangements, which meant he really needed to look hard for a job so that he could afford the monthly payments.

Chance drove out of the car dealership lot and instantly began looking for a job. There did not seem to be too many options of employment to pick from in Silver Tree Acres. The town mostly consisted of small cafés, drugstores, bars, the local post office, and a bunch of mom-and-pop shops.

Chance filled out an application for just about every store on the main strip of the small town except for the grocery store Frederick's and the old factory Constantine's.

Driving back toward the motel, Chance turned his head to the right, and there she was standing outside of the local grocery store. The blond beauty. It was as though she had this shimmering glow to her, like she was an angel. Chance couldn't take his eyes off her. That was until the sound of a loud horn coming directly at him brought his attention back to the road. Realizing he was in the wrong lane, he jerked the steering wheel as hard as he could to the right, just missing a parked car and a streetlight, then slammed on the brakes to a screeching halt.

Chance, shaking like a leaf, was too embarrassed to check the rearview mirror to see if the girl noticed his clumsiness, so he shook it off and continued his ride back to the motel. When he pulled into the parking lot of the motel, his cell phone rang. It was a job offer.

CHAPTER 18

Lena

"Hey, Bryan, I just want to say that I am very sorry if I hurt your feelings yesterday. I didn't do it intentionally. I hope you will forgive me," I said, hanging my head down, nervously kicking the dirt up with the tips of my shoes.

"Lena, I already forgot about it. I went home, kicked and screamed like a child, beat someone up...just kidding!" he said, laughing. "It is way in the past. Today is a new day, sista!" Bryan gave me a small, flirty push.

Beat someone up? That's an odd thing to say. "You really had me worried, crazy!" I said, returning the flirty push.

"Worried like you would never talk to your big brother again?" Bryan teased with a smirk on his face.

"Smart-ass!" I replied.

———

As work was winding down, Margie approached me, asking if Bryan and I would be heading over to Peeves right after work. "We sure will be."

"Great!" Margie said, a little too excited. "I am going to try and sneak out a little early so I can run home and get myself ready before seeing my *man friend* tonight."

I could not help but laugh at that statement. "Okay, Margie, we'll see you down there."

I picked up an extra shift, so when eight o'clock rolled around, I was ready to be done. There was Bryan, standing in his usual spot right outside of Frederick's front doors. I let my hair down from the ponytail that it had been in all day, shook my head, and gave myself that messy hair look I adored so much. *Not really.*

As we arrived at Peeves, Bryan held the door open for me. Once inside, I grabbed the nearest open table for two, and he went right to the bar and ordered us our first round of beers and shots of tequila to start the night off.

When Bryan sat down, we each grabbed a shot and made a toast to a good night of fun. We both cringed from the burning sensation of the tequila going down. Once the tequila kicked in, we both relaxed and began chatting about our upcoming weekend together. We discussed what we would try to do each day of our mini vacation.

After two more beers and another shot, I was ready to dance. I strolled over to the jukebox, put some money in, and as soon as "Pour Some Sugar on Me" started blaring over the speakers, my hips had a mind of their own. It was like I could no longer stand still. My body just kept moving to the beat on the makeshift dance floor. Bryan joined me shortly after, and we jumped, twisted, bent, and shook our asses for what felt like eternity.

Midnight approached quicker than anticipated, which usually happens when you are drinking alcohol, and Bryan and I stumbled out of Peeves' front door, arms around each other's necks, slurring our words while trying to say how much we loved each other and how much we looked forward to spending the long weekend together.

I just about made it all the way home before my legs started to give, and then Bryan had to practically drag me up the path to my house. I was too drunk to even be embarrassed about it. He finally just picked me up and flung me over his right shoulder like a rag doll and carried me like that the rest of the way to my house.

———

Bryan

Bryan walked into the house and placed Lena on the couch. He could not help but notice just how beautiful she was. He stood there for a couple of minutes, just looking down at her sleeping so peacefully. He wished for a moment that he could just curl up next to her on the couch but thought it would be best for him to leave. Bryan gently kissed Lena on her cheek and quietly let himself out, locking the door behind him.

As Bryan walked across the grass to his house, he thought about how nice it would be if Lena was his girlfriend and possibly willing to spend the rest of her life with him. He knew it was a long shot, but not completely out of the question. Lena did not realize how beautiful she really was, and he was the only close guy friend she had. As Bryan approached the front door to his house, he decided to not investigate these thoughts any further. The last thing he would want to do is ruin the relationship he had with Lena. If anything were to happen, it would happen. His fingertips let go of the screen to the front door, and in a whisper, the words, "I love you so much, Lena," slipped his lips before he turned and walked in the opposite direction of his house.

CHAPTER 19

Chance

"Is this Chance Wallace?" the voice on the other end of the line said.

"Yes, this is he."

"I am calling to offer you the bartending job at Wesley's, if you are still interested?"

"I say that's fantastic, and yes, I will take it. When would I start?"

"Tonight, if you're available," the voice on the other line said cheerfully.

"Great! Give me a time, and I will be there."

"If you could be here by 6:00 p.m., we can go over everything."

"Six o'clock it is then."

Chance jumped up and kicked and karate chopped the air. He was so happy. He had put so many résumés in he couldn't quite remember which of the bars Wesley's was until he arrived at the building and the big red glowing letters read "Wesley's Gentlemen's Club." *Bartending with some entertainment, not too bad,* Chance thought to himself.

"Raymond Brown," the voice from earlier on the other end of the line said, extending his hand when Chance opened the door and walked in.

"Nice to meet you, Raymond. Thanks so much for offering me this position. I am really looking forward to it," Chance said while shaking his hand.

"Oh, I bet you are," Raymond said, lowering his sunglasses and winking at Chance.

"That's not what I—"

"Nobody is judging you, son. There are no worries here" Raymond said, putting an arm around Chance's shoulders and leading him toward a door across from the bar.

Raymond got Chance set up in his office with the necessary paperwork that needed to be completed before they could begin training.

While thinking of some responses to the questions, Chance glanced around the room and noticed pictures of a variety of beautiful women hanging on the wall. One picture in particular caught his eye. The redhead with the big breasts was smiling directly at him as he quietly mouthed the words, "Holy fuck." At that same moment, Raymond walked back into the room startling him, so much that he practically jumped right out of his seat.

"I'm sorry, Chance, I didn't mean to frighten you. You always this jumpy?" Raymond joked.

"Oh, no, no, no, I just happened to see a picture of a beautiful woman hanging on your wall."

"A beautiful woman," Raymond said, laughing. "You mean beautiful women?"

"There is one in particular that caught my eye, the redhead over there," Chance said, pointing.

"Cassandra Downing. Yes, she was a rare one. She was one of the best girls I ever hired to work here. The guys loved her. That was until she was murdered recently. It's a damn shame what happened to her," Raymond said, shaking his head. "So are you ready to start?"

"Yes. Absolutely. Let's do this!" Chance replied, clapping his hands.

Raymond gave Chance a tour of the entire place, including the girls' changing room, which was empty at the time since the girls did not start until eight o'clock, the bar, and the stage area. Then Ray introduced him to Jimmy, the barback, DJ Kool, and two bouncers at the entrance, Tyler and Cheyne.

Raymond brought Chance behind the bar and gave him the lowdown of what he expected, showed him where to find everything, gave him a pat on the back, then walked away yelling, "Just have fun!" then disappeared into his office.

Chance was surprised to see the number of people pour in, especially for Silver Tree Acres being such a small town. *Well, I guess there is only so much you can do in a small town,* he thought to himself.

He was busy from the moment they opened the doors until the moment they closed at 4:00 a.m. He was so exhausted after he cleaned everything up behind the bar, he was ready to go home and crash. He didn't even have the opportunity to meet any of the girls that worked there.

"Hey, Chance, great job tonight. You really kept the drinks flowing, and I think we had some pretty satisfied customers! Did you enjoy yourself?"

"Thank you! And yes, I did enjoy myself, but man, am I whipped. I am seriously ready to go home and crash," Chance laughed.

"You don't want to hang around and have a couple drinks? On me?" Raymond joked.

"Not tonight, man. I am really beat. Can I take a rain check?"

"You will have plenty more opportunities. Don't worry about it. Today was just the first day. We have plenty more days ahead of us. Go home and get your beauty sleep, and I will see you same time tomorrow."

Chance said good night to the serious-faced bouncers, and out the front door he went.

When he got back to his room at the motel, he turned on the television as he walked toward the bathroom. While brushing his teeth, he heard the news anchorwoman's voice say, "Another woman's body was found this morning at 2:00 a.m. behind a dumpster on Watkins Avenue. The woman has not yet been identified as her body has been badly mutilated. It may take police a little while to find out who she is. Police are asking that anyone with information to please call in…" the woman's voice trailed off.

Chance was so exhausted that as soon as he laid his head on the pillow, he was out like a light.

Chapter 20

Lena

"Lena, dear, wake up!" my dad said, sounding panicked. "You have to get me to the airport in fifteen minutes."

As I slowly opened my eyes, my dad came into view, and I realized I was laying on the couch and not on my bed.

"I take it you had a late night? You couldn't even make it up to your own room, I see," he teased.

"Ha-ha, very funny, Dad! Let me just run up and take a shower, and by that time Bryan should be here."

The minute I stepped out of the shower, I heard the horn of the F-150 going off. I quickly dried myself off, got dressed, grabbed my bags, and flew down the stairs and out the front door to meet up with my dad and Bryan.

It was a long, quiet ride to the airport. You could literally cut the tension in the air with a knife. I was trying very hard not to cry, but knowing this was going to be the last moment spent with my father face-to-face for a while made it difficult. When I looked over at my dad, his eyes were swollen, and I could no longer hold back the tears. The floodgates were open.

Once we arrived at the airport, Bryan and I helped my dad check his bags, then we did a group hug that I wished could have lasted forever.

All three of us shed some tears, exchanged lots of hugs, kisses, and goodbyes, then we sadly went our separate ways. My dad and I continued to blow kisses to each other until we could no longer see each other.

I think I held myself together fairly well considering I had just said goodbye to my last living parent. I think knowing in the back of my mind that I could call my dad anytime and visit him anytime definitely helped.

"So are we ready to party?" Bryan asked excitedly as we jumped back into his truck.

"Absolutely!" I responded with a big smile on my face, wiping away the tears.

After two and a half hours of driving, we finally arrived at our destination at Sundown Valley. We first had to stop at the front desk to grab the key to our cabin, which happened to be my favorite number, 7! Then it took about twenty more minutes before arriving to the actual cabin itself. Our excitement took over, and we were bouncing around our seats in the truck like two little kids arriving at Chuck E. Cheese.

The cabin was set way back from the main road on a path with no other cabins in sight. It sat upon a small hill, hidden behind tall grass and some pine and elm trees. The entire cabin was made of wooden logs. To the left of the front door on the porch hung a beautiful wooden swing, and then dead smack in the middle of the front of the cabin sat a gorgeous bay window. When we opened the front door, the smell of apples and pine filled our noses.

To our right was a small kitchen table, and next to that were a sink, mini stove, and fridge enhanced by beautiful, handmade cupboards. There was a microwave that could fit a small plate or mug above the stove. To our left was a small living room area with a maroon-colored love seat, dark-brown leather recliner with a tall decorative lamp beside it, a bookshelf lined with books, an oak coffee table, and a television stand with no television on it. Off the living room, to the right, was a bedroom where a queen-size bed rested in the middle of the room, an antique-style lamp was perched upon a small wooden nightstand located to the left of the bed, and under a hexagon-shaped window across from the bed was a white dresser with a large oval mirror attached to it.

I looked at Bryan, and I instantly knew he was thinking the same thing I was. This was not camping at all. This was glamping!

It took us about forty-five minutes to unload and put all the stuff we brought with us away. I began cooking steaks for our first dinner there while Bryan started a fire outside for us to sit around.

When the steaks were done cooking, I brought plates outside for myself and Bryan. He was standing looking at the fire spitting to life. An ice-cold beer awaited me on the ground next to my red folding chair, which I won last year at the Silver Tree Acres fair. When we finished cleaning up after dinner, by which I mean we threw our paper plates into the fire, we relaxed in our chairs and drank our beers.

"Did you hear they found another woman's body? Mangled. I mean, isn't that crazy? Two savage murders within weeks of each other. You would almost think we had a serial killer on the loose," I said in disgust. The thought sent a chill up my spine.

"Yeah, crazy" was all Bryan shot back. "So how about a game of scat!" Bryan said, suddenly changing the subject.

There was a picnic table nearby, so the both of us grabbed an end and brought the table closer toward the fire. We played for what seemed like hours, laughing, joking, and sharing crazy stories about the people we worked with. After the fire dwindled down, we headed inside to watch the movie *Just Married* on the portable DVD player we'd brought with us.

"Should I sleep on the love seat?" Bryan asked with uncertainty in his voice.

"No, silly, the bed is big enough for the both of us to sleep on. There is no reason for you to try and squeeze yourself on the love-seat. You can have the left side of the bed. I always sleep on the right. I don't know if it is a security issue, but I have always slept on the right side of any bed, regardless of the size." At that point, I realized I must have been feeling some of the effects of the beer because I was rambling. Typically I ramble when I'm nervous.

"That is fine by me. I am just excited I don't have to try and get comfortable on a couch that is half my size. I'll take whatever side you give me," Bryan said, laughing.

Each of us took turns getting into our nightclothes then joined each other in what I believed to be a queen-size bed. It felt like such a long, eventful day, and with all the fresh air, I was whipped. Before I was comatose, I heard Bryan whisper over to me, "Sweet dreams."

———

Bryan rolled over with a huge grin on his face, feeling like he had just won the biggest lottery ever. Lying right next to Lena, he knew he would finally, for once, sleep like a baby.

CHAPTER 21

Chance

"The mutilated body found early Thursday morning was that of Sheila Johnson, 24, of Wilcox, just one town over from Silver Tree Acres…" Chance hit the snooze button. Ten minutes later, "Sheila's mother reported her missing Tuesday night after she went…"

Chance shut the alarm off before the reporter could finish her sentence.

Jeez, Chance thought to himself, *I hope this is not the norm around here, for women to go missing and get mutilated.* Chance shook his head. *Probably just a fluke.* He knew one thing for sure: he definitely had not killed this girl, because if he wasn't training at the club, he was in his motel room watching television or sleeping.

Today was going to be his first official day by himself at his new job, in a new town, with his new life. The little bit of money he had left from his old life was going toward buying some new, nicer-looking clothes in an effort to hopefully fit in tonight.

Chance got dressed, hopped in his rusty sedan, and went off toward the nearest and only shopping mall, which happened to be located in Wilcox, where the latest missing girl was from. On his way, Chance had to pass Watkins Avenue, which was still blocked off with Caution tape due to police officers and detectives still looking for clues about the murder.

Chance walked around the mall for hours trying to find some nice clothes that were reasonably priced. Express Men carried the style of clothes he was looking for, but they were way overpriced. Not having any luck at the mall, Chance decided to head back toward

Silver Tree Acres and stop at Walmart on the way. Chance ended up finding the cheap versions of the Express Men's clothes. He figured no one would even know the difference, which they would not have if he didn't forget to take all the "Exclusively at Walmart" stickers off the clothes.

———

"Hey, Chance! My man!" Raymond yelled, putting his hand on Chance's right shoulder as he walked through the back door. "Come, come and meet the beautiful girls of the night." Raymond held his hand out in front of him, leading the way. "Are you ready for tonight? It gets pretty crazy here on Friday nights," Raymond said, looking at Chance to see his reaction. Before Chance could even answer the question, Raymond started talking again, "Ah, you will be fine. Bartending is a piece of cake."

Then there they all were, scrambling around, putting on their costumes and makeup, most of them naked from the waist up. For a moment, he envisioned the big-breasted redhead running around the room getting ready to go on stage...

"Chance, did you hear me?" Raymond asked. "Are you feeling okay?"

"Yes, yes, I am fine. I'm sorry. I was just thinking about something. It's nothing, really."

"All right, then, it's showtime!" Raymond yelled, and the girls all went wild. Raymond brought an oval mirror covered with white lines over to Chance. "Here you go, buddy, since you're the newbie, you get the first hit."

"Oh, no, thank you, I don't do that." Chance waved it away.

Raymond walked around to each of the girls and let them take a hit.

Chance thought to himself, *Shit! What did I get myself into?*

As Raymond and Chance were about to leave the girls' changing room, one girl sitting off to the side in the corner by herself caught his attention. She looked so young. So innocent. He wondered how she wound up in this place. The beautiful brunette locked eyes with him for a moment before Raymond pushed him out of the changing room door.

Raymond helped Chance get prepared for the Friday-night crowd. Tonight, he was going to introduce Chance to some of the well-known faces that frequented the area.

DJ Kool waved from the booth, giving a thumbs-up before starting the music. Men and women started to pour through the doors. Chance was surprised to see how many women came there with men.

The crowd stayed steady all night long, so much so that Chance did not even get a moment to enjoy any of the performances, but before he knew it, they were already closing the doors for the night.

"The name is Bethany," a woman's voice said.

When Chance looked up, he was surprised to see the delicate brunette standing before him.

"Is that your real name or stage name?"

"That's my real name. My stage name is Bella, like the princess," Bethany giggled. "You did a real nice job tonight, cute guy." She winked and blew a kiss Chance's way before walking away toward the changing room.

Chance had a permanent smile on his face the rest of the time he cleaned up before heading home, simply due to that brief interaction.

CHAPTER 22

Lena

Morning came way too quickly. After eating breakfast, Bryan and I decided we were going to go on a picnic. We packed a basket with a blanket, a couple of sandwiches, and wine to take with us down by the lake. I ran in the bedroom to change into something a little more daring.

We're on a hill in the woods. Who is going to see us? I thought to myself.

Bryan

Bryan could not take his eyes off Lena. Her slender body was barely hidden behind a small red-and-white-plaid bikini top and dark-blue short-shorts, topped off with a pair of shiny red pumps. She did not have any makeup on, and her hair hung loosely, but to Bryan she was gorgeous regardless. He took a big gulp of air and blew it out slowly as he trailed behind her out the front door.

Being so caught up in admiring Lena, he accidently tripped over a rock on the trail as he tried to locate a spot to lay their blanket down.

"Bryan, are, are you okay?" I asked, trying very hard to keep a straight face and not laugh.

"Yes. Sorry. I was a little distracted," Bryan replied.

"How about right here?" I pointed to an area of freshly cut grass overlooking the lake, surrounded by some taller, golden, wheat-like timothy grass.

"This looks perfect," Bryan agreed, taking off his shirt and throwing it to the ground.

As Bryan was opening the bottle of wine, I lathered some sun-tan lotion on his shoulders and back. I was a little surprised at myself for never noticing how muscular Bryan was, but man, did his ripped arms and back feel amazing. While rubbing the lotion on Bryan's body, I began thinking about how I had not yet had sex with anyone, man or woman, for that fact. I guess I never really put much thought into it before today. Probably because I was always so busy with taking care of my mom while dad was away at work. As I rubbed the lotion on him, this hot, overwhelming sensation took over my body, and just as my mind started to wander, Bryan interrupted my thoughts by thanking me and handing me a glass of wine. I gracefully accepted the glass of wine and shifted my body so that I was sitting next to him rather than behind him.

"Where are my manners?" Bryan said, setting down his glass of wine. "Turn around so I can rub some lotion on you."

I inhaled my glass of wine and quickly turned so that my back was facing him. Then I had another thought and quickly sprawled myself out onto my stomach so that my entire back side was exposed.

Sipping on my third glass of wine, I was feeling no pain.

Actually, as Bryan was rubbing the lotion up and down my back, I closed my eyes to try to enjoy every movement of his hands tracing my body. I became so caught up in the moment I let out a soft moan of pleasure.

Bryan turned the opposite way and start rubbing the back of my legs with the lotion.

I felt a chill run through my body that I have never felt before, like something came alive inside of me. Bryan gently got up and lay next to me. He topped off each of our glasses of wine, and then we toasted to a wonderful friendship on a hot, sunshiny day. After throwing back our drinks, we gradually began leaning in toward each other. Next thing I knew, we were passionately making out. Both of our bodies began to intertwine into a hot, sweaty knot. I could feel Bryan's manhood, *If that's even a word*, against my body. Curiosity getting the best of me, I leaned in to explore the hard object. As one of my hands was caressing his fullness, my other hand took his hand and guided it straight to the wetness that continued to escape from me down below, so much so that I felt that I couldn't even control it. *What is this amazing feeling?* I thought to myself. *All from the touch of his fingers? Wow!* My body involuntarily began grinding against Bryan's erect penis. Neither of us could resist the temptation any longer. We quickly began to undress each other, stripping off piece by piece until our hot, sweaty bodies were completely naked and directly up against each other. With my right hand, I lead him into the hot, wet, swollen area between my legs. Soon enough, our bodies felt like they became one.

Oh boy, I thought to myself. *Painful, but at the same time it felt good. It is a good painful!* Before either of us could remotely realize what was actually happening, we both climaxed at the exact same time. Two seconds after pulling our sweaty bodies apart, we were taken aback by some kids riding by on their bikes, yelling, just on the opposite side of the hill we were on. Bryan and I looked at each other and mouthed the words "Oh my god" before bursting out into laughter while desperately trying to put our clothes back on quickly.

"Well, that was definitely not the type of picnic I had in mind, but it was definitely the best picnic I have ever had," Bryan said, followed by a nervous giggle.

"Um, me either," I replied nervously with my head down.

I guess we got a little carried away in the moment. With what had just taken place, I thought I would feel differently. I was not really sure how I thought I'd feel, but I thought something would feel different. Not that it was bad, it just seemed as though something was missing. Regardless of how I felt, Bryan had a huge smile that could brighten up the entire sky, like a boy who just got laid for the first time. *Oh wait! He is a boy who just got laid for the first time, silly,* I thought to myself.

"Here, let me help you with that," Bryan said, reaching toward the back of me to help fasten my bikini top.

After we finished getting dressed, we figured we should eat the food we brought with us before heading back to the cabin.

Chapter 23

Chance

Chance could feel the warmth of the sun upon his face. He turned his head toward the wall and slowly opened his eyes so that they could adjust to how bright it was in his room. When he turned and looked at the clock, it was already one in the afternoon. *This is going to be quite an adjustment*, Chance thought to himself.

Chance rolled out of bed, still groggy, and threw on the pair of jeans he had worn the night before. When he reached in his pocket, there it was, written neatly on a napkin, "Bethany, 797-6057." It made him smile. After staring at it for a while and realizing his shift didn't start for another six hours, he dialed the number before he could change his mind.

"Hello?" said a soft voice.

"Hi! Can I speak to Bethany?" Chance asked, then held his breath with his fist in his mouth.

"This is she. Who is this?" Bethany asked.

"It's Chance—"

And before he could finish his sentence, Bethany cut him off, "Oh my gosh! Hi! I can't believe you called." Then it sounded as though the phone was being covered, then some mumbling, and then footsteps.

"Hello? Hello? are you still there?" she asked in a hush-hush voice.

"I am so sorry, did I interrupt something? I'm so—" and she cut him off again.

"No, you didn't interrupt anything at all. I was just gathering myself trying to get comfortable." If only Chance had known that she had really just finished sucking one guy's dick while getting fucked in the ass at the same time by another, he would not have thought twice about even reaching out to her, but he did not know, so at the time he was happy to hear her voice.

"I was thinking maybe we could meet up for lunch or some-thing. I am still fairly new in town, so I don't really know anyone."

"Sure, that sounds great! Where would you like to meet?" Bethany asked.

"Are you familiar with Kitty's Café? We could meet there?" Chance asked, waiting on a response as to whether or not she knew the place.

"That sounds perfect. Let me take a quick shower, and I will meet you there by two fifteen?" When Chance responded that he would gladly be there, she hung up the phone, grabbed the money from the two men, kicked them out of her hotel room, and did exactly what she said she was going to do—hop in the shower.

———

Right at 2:15 p.m., she walked through the door of Kitty's Cafe. It was hard for Chance not to stare. She had an amazing body. He was not positive if her boobs were real, but they were large and perfectly round, and he could see her nipples showing through her white fitted T-shirt. And her butt, wow, looked exactly like Kim Kardashian's. Big and round. Her cheeks hung right below the bottoms of the jean shorts, just a little sneak peek.

"Everything is real," she said as she sat down.

"I'm sorry, what?" Chance asked, taken off guard.

"My tits and ass. I assume that is what you were staring at as I made my way over here."

"Guilty as charged," Chance said, putting his hands up in the air, smiling, and looking down toward the ground, slightly embar-rassed. "I apologize, I didn't realize it was that obvious—my staring, that is."

"Well, I apologize too," Bethany said back.

"For what? You didn't do anything," Chance said, confused.

"But I did do something. I lied."

"About what?"

"My boobs and butt. They're not real. They're totally fake. I wish they were my own, but unfortunately, my mom did not bless me with boobs or a butt when she had me." Bethany giggled like a schoolgirl, her cheeks turning pink.

"That's okay. Fake. Real. Who cares? It's all the same." Chance laughed back. "I like big butts and I cannot lie...Sorry, sorry, it was like perfect timing, I couldn't help myself." Chance grinned, also blushing.

"You are cute, sweet, and funny. You don't normally find that combination in guys. It's extremely rare," Bethany said, leaning into the table toward him.

Chance couldn't help but think this move was on purpose, so of course his eyes drifted downward toward her cleavage.

"So how did a pretty girl like you get wound up in stripping?"

"I've been doing it since I was in high school. It's super easy money, and I actually enjoy dancing."

"High school?" Chance blurted out, sounding a little rude, but not intentionally. He was just surprised that she started so young.

"If you want to live the good life and must pay for your education at the same time, this is the way to go. Like I said, the money is quick and easy," Bethany responded matter-of-factly.

Just then their food arrived. And although Chance knew that Bethany was not purposely trying to look seductive while eating her french fries, she did. Then as she took the first bite of her double cheeseburger, a drip consisting of ketchup and mustard fell upon her left breast. She gently set down her double cheeseburger, looked down at her breast, and when she looked up, she had a serious face when she asked, "Would you like to lick it off?"

"Here?" Chance asked, almost choking on his food.

"Of course not, silly," Bethany responded, laughing. "Let's take our food to go."

CHAPTER 24

Lena

Arriving back at the cabin, I wasn't sure whether to say anything about what had just taken place or just pretend like it didn't happen. Bryan seemed to be fine. Jolly, even. Maybe I should just try to forget that it happened, but how? We just had sex together for the very first time, and I am pretty positive we both just lost our virginity. That is, unless there was something Bryan hadn't told me. I couldn't help but wonder if this would change things between us. Hopefully, if so, it would not be for the worst.

I loved Bryan dearly, but in a different type of way. I hoped I didn't just make the biggest mistake of my life, or his for that fact.

"Shower!" Bryan shouted.

"Me and you? Together?" I asked, panicking.

"No, jumpy girl, I was just letting you know that I was heading into the shower before we made dinner plans and settled down."

"Right...I knew that," I mumbled to myself, taking in a deep breath and letting it out slowly. As Bryan showered, I decided to lay down on the chocolate-colored recliner to relax. I must have fallen into a sound sleep because when I woke up, the cabin was dark, and Bryan was already in bed. As I slipped into my PJs and snuck into bed, Bryan whispered, "You were sleeping so soundly and looked so peaceful I didn't have the heart to wake you. I hope you don't mind, I just threw together a small meal for dinner and had a couple of beers. I thought maybe tomorrow we could take a hike through the woods. What do you think?"

"I think that sounds amazing! Thank you for letting me sleep. I apparently needed it."

I wasn't absolutely positive what to expect once I got into bed next to Bryan. I let out a huge sigh of relief when I snuggled under the covers and realized that Bryan had sweatpants on. I really didn't understand why I was so on edge.

When I turned onto my side, Bryan scooted over and spooned me, but I was okay with it. He made me feel safe.

Within minutes, we were fast asleep.

———

The next morning, I woke up feeling extremely sore down below, which then brought me back to the moment from yesterday on the picnic blanket.

Okay, I told myself, *don't get all crazy and weirded out now, as we planned to hike today. I must keep it together for both of our sakes.*

"As long as it's okay with you, I think I'll go shower before breakfast and heading out on our hike," I said it in such a tone that it sounded like I was asking permission.

"No problem," Bryan replied, winking his right eye. "Breakfast shall be served when you get back, madam," he said, bowing down, making the both us laugh.

"Bryan, you don't have to do that."

"Bow?" he asked jokingly. "I know, I know, but I want to," he said with a sly grin on his face.

Of course now my mind started to read into his grin, as if his grin was implying something different than just being a grin. *Oh, this is foolish,* I thought to myself. *I need to get a grip, or the rest of this trip won't be much fun.*

When I arrived back at the cabin, Bryan had an entire smorgasbord of food laid out on the kitchen table for the two of us. Eggs, sausage, pancakes, bacon, toast—you name it, we had it.

"Wow, you really went all out," I said, trying not to sound too surprised.

"Sure did! Was kind of hungry and figured we would need as much energy as possible to do all of the climbing and walking today." We both sat down.

"Hey. What do you think about hitting up the local joint here later? Maybe do a little dancing, have a couple of shots, act like crazy fools?" Bryan suggested while munching on his food.

I looked up at Bryan with a mouth full of food and a big grin. "That sounds like a lot of fun."

After cleanup, we headed out toward one of the trails that surrounded our cabin.

We briskly walked past tall trees into the silent wilderness. It was so serene. The eerie silence of the open forest floor gave me what almost felt like a natural high.

We walked up and down hills, over rocks, and through river bends. At one point, we had to walk along a slanted hill next to the river. It gave me a sudden rush, similar to what I had felt during intercourse with Bryan yesterday. The tingling sensation actually felt good and made me wonder if it was a sign that my body enjoyed what happened yesterday.

Suddenly, I was brought back to reality when my foot slid on one of the wet rocks.

"Lena!" Bryan yelped as he grabbed my wrist and caught me before I completely lost my balance.

"I'm sorry, I guess my mind drifted off. I'll be much more careful," I said, feeling kind of stupid.

"Lena, it's okay. What do you think I'm going to do, scold you?"

With that, we looked at each other and started laughing hysterically.

About four hours passed before we made our way out of the forest and back to civilization.

"That was really fun," I said to Bryan, smiling.

"Sure was, but now, my friend," Bryan said with a Southern drawl, rubbing his hands together, "it's time to go get ready so that we can get some grub and have some fun!"

Back at the cabin, we both grabbed our towels and shower stuff then headed off in the direction of the respective shower stalls to get all the sweaty grime off our bodies.

When we met back up at the cabin, I couldn't help but notice Bryan taking in a deep breath, like he had smelled something amazing in the air.

The only thing I could assume it was that he was smelling was my wild berry shampoo. However, the only thing I could smell was the Axe body wash Bryan must have doused himself with.

Five minutes later, we were hopping in Bryan's F-150, heading toward town.

CHAPTER 25

Chance

On the drive to his place, Chance kept turning his head to look at the drip still resting upon Bethany's breast.

"Don't worry, cowboy, it'll still be there once we get to our destination. Keep your eyes on the road."

Chance was hard as a rock and just wanted to pull over and rip her clothes off right then and there. *Five more minutes, five more minutes*, Chance kept repeating in his head.

As soon as they pulled into the parking lot of his apartment complex, Chance practically jumped out of the driver's seat before the car was fully parked. He ran to the passenger side of the car, opened the door, and yanked on Bethany's arm to hurry her out of the car.

"Chance! The food!" she kidded.

"Screw the food. That drip on your chest will fill me up."

Chance unlocked the door to his apartment and pulled Bethany in.

"First, I just need to do this." Chance grabbed both boobs and squeezed them together as if he was going to motorboat them, but instead he took his warm tongue and soft lips and French-kissed the tops of her breasts.

As soon as his lips moved away from her breasts, they both began clawing at each other's clothes. Bethany squatted down and began unzipping Chance's pants and was very impressed by what greeted her.

"Wow, lover boy!" was all she said before sucking him off, hard.

Chance was in a world of ecstasy. It had been so long since a girl had gone down on him. He'd almost forgotten what it felt like.

Bethany, starting from below, kissed him all the way up his body until she got to his mouth, where she then ferociously kissed him. Then she bit his lip and pushed him down onto the bed and slid herself on top of him.

Oh my fucking god! Chance thought to himself. *Is this chick for real?* He could not believe how wet she was. Right after that thought, he couldn't hold it any longer, and they both climaxed at the same time.

As Bethany was getting dressed, Chance just lay on his bed, staring at the ceiling.

"That was fucking amazing," he said out loud.

"Glad you liked it. I have to run, though, and get ready for work," Bethany mumbled as she put her shirt back on. "See you in a few hours," she said as she walked out of his apartment, winking at him before she disappeared behind the door.

"Wait!" Chance jumped off the bed and ran to the door naked, swinging it open, and yelling, "I have to drive you home!" but his voice trailed off in the distance once he realized she was nowhere to be seen.

Where the hell did she go so fast? he wondered.

———

Chance made sure he wore his best-looking outfit from Walmart to impress his lady. Soon, he would be able to afford a nice wardrobe, but for now, these clothes had to suffice.

Chance pulled into the parking lot of Wesley's, where a few cars were already parked. When Chance walked in, there were a couple of girls standing around, but he walked straight to the bar to get things ready for the night. Then he heard some noise coming from Ray's office. *Huh, I didn't see Ray's car out there. Maybe he got dropped off,* Chance thought to himself. Ignoring the sound, he continued to get everything ready behind the bar before the front doors were opened. That's when Chance heard another loud noise coming from Ray's office, and it sounded like someone yelled. Chance left from behind the bar and walked toward Ray's office to make sure everything was okay. He was not prepared for what he was about to see.

"Holy shit! Are you fucking kidding me?" Chance yelled at the top of his lungs, scaring the shit out of Bethany and the two men, one of which was behind banging her from behind and the other who had his penis in her mouth.

"Chance, what the hell are you doing in here?" Bethany yelled back. "You can't just barge into rooms without" Bethany did not get to finish her sentence as Chance cut her off.

"This is Ray's office! I'm sorry, I was worried that someone was being hurt with all the damn loud noises coming from in here. What the hell was I thinking. Seriously." Chance grabbed his hair.

"Chance, you can't tell me that you thought you and I were..." Bethany trailed off. "I told you I needed to make money." She reached her hand out toward Chance.

"Don't fucking touch me," Chance growled.

"Hey, whoa, what's going on over here?" Ray asked, putting his arm around Chance's neck like they were old friends. Ray took one look at Chance and knew something was wrong. He looked like he was ready to hurt somebody. Ray was not aware of the afternoon tryst with Chance and Bethany, but he definitely knew Chance needed to cool off. The crazy look in his eyes worried Ray.

"Hey, buddy. Why don't you take tonight off? I can handle it. Go someplace and cool off, have a drink, and when you come back, please make sure you have it together, okay? I don't need any more problems than I already have. Can you do that?" Ray asked with his hand still on Chance's shoulder.

"Whatever," Chance said as he pushed Ray's hand off his shoulder and stormed out of the club.

CHAPTER 26

Lena

After a twenty-minute drive, we pulled into a parking lot in front of a small hole-in-the-wall called Jebbs. There was a pretty decent amount of people inside of the bar, especially for it being a Sunday.

"You go ahead and grab us a seat, and I'll go grab us a couple of drinks," Bryan said as he held the door open for me.

I went and found a small round table not too far from the jukebox. While I sat at the table waiting, I looked around, taking in my surroundings. The crowd consisted of a few older people, some middle-aged, and a couple of young adults. They all probably lived in the area. It was a new, refreshing scene from what we were used to. As I was smiling, taking it all in, Bryan strolled over with two beers and two shots.

"Got our usual," Bryan said with a silly half smile on his face. "Cheers to a great night!"

We held our shot glasses up to our lips and tipped them back until the warm liquid hit the backs of our throats.

"Nothing like a good ole snakebite to start the night out," I said, making a pucker face. Then we both took a swig of our beer to wash it down.

"You missed your mouth a little" Bryan said, with a funny look on his face.

"I did that on purpose, did you not know that?" I said jokingly, then wiped my mouth and smeared it on the side of his face.

"So I was thinking...what if you and I..." Bryan paused for a moment before finishing his sentence. "What if we moved in together? I mean, we are with each other every day. Nothing would really be that much different than it is now, I mean, aside from us waking up in the same house."

At first, I just peered at him, not really sure if he was actually serious or not. I was waiting for him to say "Just kidding" or "I'm just messing around."

"Your silence is very reassuring," he giggled nervously.

"Oh! You are serious! Oh my god, I am sorry. I literally thought you were joking, but you are not joking, are you? I'm sorry, I'm such a jerk, that came out wrong. You just took me by surprise. It's a big decision to make. I'd have to think about it."

I hoped that he couldn't make out the nervousness in my voice as I responded.

"No decision needs to be made today. I just thought we could be, like, roomies, ya know? Now that your dad is gone, I thought maybe I could take care of you," he offered.

"Bryan, no offense, but I'm a big girl who can take care of herself. Not that I'm saying no because I'm not, but I do need some time to think about it. On that note, want another beer?"

Three beers and two snakebites later, I was feeling amazing, like I could float, which in return made me feel like dancing. I walked over to the jukebox and popped in some one-dollar bills, and suddenly Tears for Fears's "Everybody Wants to Rule the World" started playing loudly over the speakers. I couldn't help but start moving my hips. Eighties music was a secret obsession of mine.

I did an electric-slide-type move back to our table, and Bryan stood up. He grabbed my hands, and we began busting a move with the music. It felt as though it was just the two of us in our own little world, dancing like crazy, when in reality all eyes were on us. At that instant nothing seemed to matter. It felt as though everything was frozen in time.

Then "One Headlight" by the Wallflowers began playing. Bryan wrapped his arms gently around my shoulders and mine moved to his waist. Our bodies swayed slowly to the music, and when I lifted my head to look up at Bryan, our eyes locked. When our lips touched, it felt so right we became lost in the moment. It was so passionate. While our tongues were gently exploring each other, I felt a rush of heat derive from my toes all the way up my body. We were so caught up in the moment we almost forgot we were in a bar full of people until some man at the end of the bar yelled, "Get a room!" That caught our attention.

Bryan and I looked at each other, blushing with embarrassment and slowly moving apart from each other, giggling like two little elementary-school kids who had just experienced their very first kiss ever.

"I'm going to the ladies' room," I said, hanging my head but smiling.

"And I'll go get the next round!" Bryan yelled as I made my way toward the bathroom.

As I exited the bathroom, I noticed a big-busted Dolly Parton–looking blonde lean over toward Bryan at the bar, and I took a step back so that I wasn't in their view, and I overheard her say, "You two must be newly engaged or just married." Bryan turned toward her with a smile on his face and responded, "Nope, we're just really close friends, that's all."

With a surprise look on her face, she replied, "Wow, that's some really, *really*, good friends. With benefits, I hope. At least for your sake anyway, cowboy!"

"Someday maybe we'll be more than friends," Bryan replied while making air quotes with his fingers.

On the way back to our table, I couldn't help but tease him. "Looks like you met a friend," I said, winking.

"Yeah, you know how those older women love me!" he joked, puffing out his chest.

"I challenge you to a dance off, Mr. Bryan Mills!" I said, pointing at him.

"Oh! It's on!" he teased back.

The words of "Pour Some Sugar on Me" started to fill the bar, and the both of us danced crazily. I tried twerking to be funny, but

I think I looked more like someone convulsing and trying to hop backward on my tiptoes.

Then I lost my balance and fell into some guy, spilling his own beer all down the front of him.

"Oh my god, oh my god, I'm soooooo sorry," I apologized over and over, covering my mouth with my hands. "I'm such a klutz. Are you okay? Let me help you with that." I nervously reached for some napkins. While reaching for the napkins, I tripped over my foot and literally fell headfirst right into the guy's chest.

"Whoa, whoa, easy there, tiger," I heard a deep voice say as I raised my head in complete embarrassment.

"I'm sorry, I'm so embarrassed, I didn't even see you there," I began to say when he laughed.

"How could you possibly have seen me? You were literally hopping backwards."

"I was twerking!" I said, holding a finger up in the air, like I had just made a valid point of some sort.

"Oh, is that what you call that?" The guy laughed under his breath.

When I looked up, we held each other's gaze for a second.

CHAPTER 27

Chance

Chance was furious. He couldn't believe what he'd just witnessed. The image of her and those guys kept playing over and over in his head. *She's a stripper. I should've known better. Seriously, what was I thinking?* Chance laughed to himself, hitting the steering wheel. The first bar he came upon would be the one where he would wallow in his pain for being so stupid.

I need to clear my head. I need to figure out what I want to do with my life. I miss Amanda. I miss my friends. I miss my family. But I can't go back. Sadly, I have to move forward and put that life in the past.

His cell phone began to ring, and when he noticed who was calling, he pulled over and parked his car.

"Hey, handsome! How's it going? I miss you!" Leeza said. Chance could hear the smile in her voice.

"You must've been reading my mind. I literally was just thinking about you."

"How's the new life going?"

"It's okay. Still a huge adjustment. I found a job, so hopefully that'll help me get up on my feet again. It sucks being poor and having no friends or family to visit."

"Don't you worry, I'll definitely come visit, that is, once you invite me!" Leeza teased.

"You can come any time your little heart desires, unless I'm hooking up with a hot chick at the time," he joked.

"Oh, so it's like that, huh? You a big playa now, Mr. Tough Guy?"

"No, I wish. I've had a couple hookups here and there, but nothing serious at all. Just trying to lay low and keep myself out of trouble, 'cause you know how much trouble I can make," Chance said jokingly. He was actually the complete opposite of a trouble-maker, at least he thought so.

"Soooo where are you working?"

"Okay, don't be judgmental. I just took the job because it was the first place to call me back and make an offer."

"All right, is it like Walgreens or something? Just tell me. You know I'd never judge you or your decisions."

"You promise?"

"I promise."

"The place is called Wesley's. It's a strip club."

"A strip club?" Leeza said, sounding surprised.

"You said you wouldn't judge!"

"I'm not judging, I just said 'a strip club,' that's all. You have to do what you have to do to make ends meet. I get it. When I come there to visit, are you going to dance for me?" Leeza teased.

"No, of course not! I'm not a stripper. I'm just working as a bartender at the club. Girl, are you out of your mind?" Chance replied, laughing.

"Hey, I didn't know. You just said you were working at a strip club. You never said what you were doing there." Leeza snickered.

"It's so great to hear a familiar voice. I miss you. I also keep thinking about Amanda."

"Boy, you need to let that shit go!" Leeza quipped. "I do have to run, though. You take care of yourself. I will try and come visit as soon as I can. I miss you too. And please, whatever you do, do *not* sleep with any of the strippers. They have all kinds of diseases you don't be knowing about! Be smart, use your head, and I'm talking about the one on your shoulders!" She added, "Hopefully, I'll see you soon. Hey, by the way, do they have any cute guys up there?" They both became silent, so much so that you could almost hear the crickets chirping. Leeza busted out laughing, breaking the silence. "Ha-ha, just kidding. Have a good night, sweetie," she said before hanging up the phone.

Chance tossed his phone on the passenger seat and pulled back onto the road. Not even ten minutes later, he found a bar and pulled into the parking lot.

CHAPTER 28

Chance

Holy crap! The blond-haired, blue-eyed beauty was standing there right in front of him. He couldn't believe his eyes. *Who would've thought of all the places to be that she would be here, in the middle of nowhere?*

———

Lena

I went up to the bar and held up two fingers, trying to shout over the loud music playing, "Snakebites, please!"

As I made my way back to our table, I couldn't help but notice the gentleman whom I made spill his drink all over himself sitting in the corner all alone. He looked kind of lost.

I heard Bryan snickering as I approached our table.

"Lena, that was quite a show you put on there!" Bryan couldn't help himself. He busted out laughing, so hard that he snorted, bringing my attention back to him.

"Stop laughing," I said, nudging him. "That was all part of my plan." Bryan laughed even harder. "Life would be so boring without me, remember that," I said, wiggling my finger in his face. Then with a pouty face, I said, "I feel really bad for spilling that man's drink all over him. He came out of nowhere. And he seems so…sad."

"Really, Lena? Since when do you feel sad for strangers?"

"Ha-ha, very funny, smarty-pants."

When Bryan got up and started walking toward the men's room, I decided to take the opportunity to go apologize to the lonely-looking, deep-voiced stranger that was wearing his own beer because of me.

"Is this seat taken?" I asked, pointing to the chair across from him.

"Is that supposed to be some kind of joke?" the deep voice asked with one eyebrow cocked.

"No, no, I'm sorry. I didn't mean to bother you. I just feel really bad about earlier, and I'd like to buy you your next drink," I stammered. I was not sure what it was about the deep-voiced stranger in front of me, but he unexpectedly gave me the chills, but in a good way.

"Would you like a shot?" I asked as my buzz was slowly fizzling.

"If it's a snakebite, absolutely not!" He dragged those last two words. At first, I was a little taken aback, but then he smiled at me. "I will just take that beer you offered me, if that is okay with you, ma'am."

I wasn't really sure why I was so comfortable talking to this stranger, but I went on to explain to him why I did snakebite shots, and I think I caught him off guard.

"It's the only shot I can seem to handle, sadly," I started.

"Come again?"

I immediately felt stupid for telling this stranger something I knew he probably couldn't care less about. Then he surprised me.

"It's okay, everyone has different taste. There's nothing to be ashamed of. However, it'd be a different story if we were talking about your little dance you did earlier."

We both laughed at that, which put me a little more at ease.

"On that note, I'm walking away, and one beer is coming up!" I hopped out of the seat and headed for the bar.

"Hey, chicka, you ready to wrap things up?" Bryan asked, leaning into me at the bar.

"Sure, I just want to get that gentleman a beer since I spilled his first one on him."

I walked back over to where the deep-voiced stranger was sitting. "Here you go, kind sir. Sorry for all the craziness." I saluted and handed him his beer.

"Thank you, pretty lady. The name is Chance."

I stopped in my tracks as I headed toward the door. "Good night then, Chance!" And with a pivot of my foot and a big smile on my face, I caught up to Bryan, and we drunkenly wavered out of the bar together.

On our way to the truck, I realized that when the deep-voiced stranger said his name, I had felt a very strange sensation, like butterflies in my stomach. I brushed the thought away. *Who gets butterflies in their stomach when a stranger introduces himself? Good Lord, Lena, get a grip!* I must've had one too many drinks or shots—or both, for that matter.

"Earth to Lena," I heard Bryan say with a little 'tude in his voice. "Lena, you just walked right past the truck. You feel okay?"

"Whoops, my bad. Apparently I'm already in la-la land. Need sleep! Let's go home!" I said in a zombie-like voice.

CHAPTER 29

Lena

As Bryan and I spooned each other on the bed, my mind drifted back to the bar, to the corner where the deep-voiced man was sitting. "The name is Chance," I heard him say. Then my eyes opened, and I sat up in a flash, realizing I'd never even introduced myself! Bryan must've been sleeping like a rock as he didn't even budge from my disturbance. With a swift smack to the head with the palm of my hand, I mumbled "Idiot" to myself. Then I lay back down and fell asleep.

"I really hate packing up to go home," I whined. "And it doesn't help having a horrific headache on top of doing it. However, I did sleep like a baby!"

"You definitely were sound asleep! I snuggled you to death, and you didn't even budge. You were as stiff as a log!" Bryan said jokingly.

If only he knew I was the one who jolted upright and he was actually the one that didn't budge.

Sheryl Crow's "Every Day Is a Winding Road" played on the radio as we headed home. I stared out the window along the road we were traveling on and wondered if my mom was looking down on me. I literally had no idea what my future would turn out to be like, but I hoped it would be one that my mother would be proud of.

I began to think about what Bryan had asked me at the bar last night about moving in together. *I wonder if Bryan might be my soul mate. How can I tell?* I looked up toward the sky hoping for some kind of sign from my mom. "Silly girl," I said under my breath.

"Hey, lost in translation, you are awfully quiet over there. Is everything okay?" Bryan asked, interrupting my thoughts.

"I'm fine. I guess I was just daydreaming," I said, smiling at Bryan.

"We have to stop soon to get gas. Would you like to grab something to eat?" he asked, looking over at me.

"Sure!" I replied, upbeat.

After Bryan parked the truck, we hopped out and made our way over to a little café called Edgar's. The place was packed and smelled of delicious greasy food. Once we placed our food order, Bryan grabbed both of my hands and pulled them toward him, then he asked me if I had put in any thought about moving in together.

"I did," I replied and then looked up toward the sky. *Mom? Anything?* Just when I was about to answer, I heard the deep voice from the night before right behind me. Quickly, without thinking, I pulled my hands from Bryan's and turned to see Chance sitting in a booth by himself, talking up the waitress.

"I never introduced myself," I mumbled, not realizing I'd said it out loud until I heard Bryan ask, "I'm sorry, what'd you say?" sounding all confused.

"I never told Chance my name last night at the bar," I said slowly, as if I had to think hard about it.

"Why does it even matter whether or not you told him your name?" Bryan again sounded very confused and a little agitated.

Next thing I knew, I was up and walking toward Chance while Bryan was sitting there stunned, thinking we were going to have this beautiful moment about our future moving-in plans.

"Lena," I said, extending out my hand toward Chance. "It's Lena," I repeated.

Then these gorgeous green eyes looked up at me, and I felt my heart skip a beat.

"I forgot to introduce myself last night."

"Well, nice to meet you then, Lena. I hope you didn't lose any sleep over that." Chance chuckled.

I suddenly felt foolish remembering my reaction the night before.

CHAPTER 30

Lena

I didn't know it, but Chance couldn't believe his luck of running into me twice in two days—and now he knew my name.

"Do you live around here?" I asked, breaking the awkward silence and uncomfortable eye contact. But before Chance answered the question, he tilted his head to the side and looked past me, over at Bryan, who was staring directly at us.

"Um, your boyfriend doesn't look too keen on you being over here. I think he's trying to set me on fire with his eyes," Chance said with a little laugh, looking back and forth from me to Bryan.

I looked back at Bryan, and with a wave of my hand in his direction, I laughed and said, "Oh, no, that's *not* my boyfriend. That's my best friend Bryan."

Chance exhaled with a look of relief on his face then answered my question, "No, actually, I don't live around here. I was just passing through." He paused. "I think your food may have arrived because your friend is trying to wave you down."

"Okay, well, enjoy your meal! I just wanted to make sure you knew my name. I'm so glad I ran into you again. Good day to you and your travels."

Good day to you and your travels? What an idiot. I must've sounded ridiculous. Who says that? I thought to myself, slightly shaking my head as I turned and walked back toward Bryan.

"So it seems as though you made a new friend," Bryan said, looking quizzically at me.

"Very funny. I just felt really bad that I never introduced myself to him last night," I said defensively.

"Why do you even care? He's a stranger that you're never going to see again." Bryan shrugged before shoving pancakes down his throat. "Didn't your parents teach you never to talk to strangers?" Bryan couldn't help but laugh hysterically at his own wisecrack.

"As a matter of fact, they did teach me never to talk to strangers, but if you remember correctly, we met last night, so technically he is not a stranger!" I replied, taking a bite of my breakfast sandwich.

"Do you feel better now that you got that off of your chest?"

"Yes, actually, I do. He seems so out of his element."

"Why does that matter?" Bryan asked, again sounding agitated.

"It doesn't matter. I was just trying to make conversation. You know what, let's change the subject please."

"Yes, let's go back to before you were so distracted by a stranger," Bryan said. "Me moving in, have you thought about it?"

"I did think about it, and yeah, I think it'd be fun! I say let's give it a try," I responded enthusiastically.

"That's my girl!" Bryan said, beaming from ear to ear and reaching over the table to give me a high five.

CHAPTER 31

Bryan

"What do you say about having movie night when we get back home?"

When there was no response, Bryan looked over to see that Lena was fast asleep in the passenger seat. He couldn't help but take in the profile of the beautiful features of Lena's face. Her skin looked so soft, so pale, and her blond hair brushed gently across her face with the breeze that crept through the crack in the window. Bryan turned the radio low and let Lena rest. While driving, he began to wonder what life would be like marrying her and raising a family together. To him, she was his soul mate. He didn't see other girls the way he saw Lena. Then again, he never really put forth effort to get to know any other girls.

The moment they'd shared together the other day meant the world to Bryan, especially that he was Lena's first. He didn't want to bring it up or discuss it because it was so sudden and unexpected. He didn't want to take any chances of upsetting her or ruining the memory of it. He did kind of wish Lena would have said something about that day, that moment. Hopefully, she didn't regret it. He preferred to think she didn't talk about it because she wanted to savor the moment. That thought brought a smile to his face.

Lena

"What are you so smiley about over there?" I asked, apparently startling Bryan as he jumped at the sound of my voice.

"Lena, hey, good morning, sunshine. How was that nap of yours? I was just thinking about the move and how excited I am about it, that's all." Bryan reached over and tickled my side as he responded. "How about a good scary movie tonight like *My Bloody Valentine* or even *The Hills have Eyes*?" he asked.

"Sounds like a perfect night to me!" I replied excitedly.

As we pulled up to the front of the house, got out of the truck, and unloaded everything we took on our mini getaway, it began to rain. Just as we stepped through the front door, the rain came down in buckets followed by loud cracks of thunder and flashes of lightning that lit up the entire sky.

"This is such a perfect scary movie night!" I squealed, rubbing my palms together and flashing a witchy grin at Bryan. Then I challenged, "Whoever gets dressed and back to the couch first doesn't have to make the popcorn or get the drinks!"

"Oh, it's on!" Bryan yelled back, accepting the challenge.

Then off we both went, running up the stairs to see who could get dressed the fastest. Once we reached the top of the stairs and I ran toward my room, Bryan realized his clothes were still packed in a bag downstairs.

"This is so not fair!" Bryan yelled. "You tricked me! You knew I had no clothes ready to change into!"

As Bryan ran back down the stairs, I was in my room quickly changing and giggling to myself. When I finished changing, I ran back down the stairs, heading toward the couch in the front room, when Bryan tackled and started tickling me.

"You're such a cheater," he growled.

"Too bad so sad. You lost! You get to make the popcorn! I'll be nice and get the movie ready."

"Fine," Bryan grunted, walking toward the kitchen.

While Bryan was getting everything together in the kitchen, I put *The Hills Have Eyes* into the DVD player and lit a bunch of candles around the front room. I turned off all the lights, grabbed a blanket, and lay down on the couch.

I popped my head over the couch when I heard Bryan's footsteps getting closer.

"You realize we're seriously like two little kids, don't you?"

I just nodded my head yes in agreement to that statement, with a big ole cheesy smile on my face.

"Cheers to a new chapter of us!" Bryan said, holding up his glass of pop.

"Cheers!" I chimed in and clanked my glass of pop against his.

CHAPTER 32

Chance

Buzz. Buzz.

Chance could not understand why his alarm would be going off so early in the morning. He didn't need to get up for several more hours.

When he lifted his head from the pillow to hit the alarm clock, he realized it wasn't the alarm at all. Someone was ringing his doorbell.

What the fuck! Who could possibly be here at eight o'clock in the morning?

"Hold on! I am coming!" Chance yelled, stumbling around trying to pull his pants on.

"What's so important that couldn't wait—" Chance's voice drifted off as he opened the door.

"Hey, handsome!" Leeza yelled, grabbing him around the neck and nearly suffocating him. "Wow, look at you! Nice six-pack, arms are looking good, and looks like someone down below is happy to see me," she said, grabbing his junk.

"Hey, whoa, okay, I just woke up. This is totally natural for men when they wake up. You wouldn't know this because you always kick the guys out right after sex, so they never get to see the light of day at your place!" Chance said, squinting from the bright sun.

"You should really take a shower, bud. I don't want to come off as being mean, but you look like your head and pillow were in a wrestling match."

"Ha-ha, very funny, Leeza. Get over here and give me a fucking hug. Holy shit. I can't believe you're here. No cops followed you, right?" Chance grabbed her by the arms, yanking her to his chest and squeezing her.

"No, jackass. No cops followed me here. I think you're in the clear anyways. There hasn't been much chatter around the town about you. On the spur of the moment, I decided that I wanted to come and surprise you! So are you surprised?" Leeza asked with her head tilted and hand on her hip.

"Extremely surprised. We just talked on the phone yesterday. Here, let me get dressed we can go grab a bite to eat," Chance said, grabbing some of his clothes and heading toward the bathroom.

"Wait!" Leeza said, holding her arm out, expecting Chance to grab her hand.

"I was hoping that maybe we could take care of your little, or should I say big, problem below. We wouldn't want that to go to waste now, would we?" Leeza said, winking.

"Leeza, you were my fiancée's best friend, I..." his voice trailed off.

"Shhh," Leeza said, placing her fingers over his mouth. "She's gone, and I'm going to be honest with you. I have not had sex in, like, three months."

"So you basically want to be friends...but...with benefits?" Chance asked, a little unsure if that was where she was going with it.

"Just for the time I am here. That's all. If that's okay with you? You told me you weren't serious with anyone." Leeza looked at him, waiting for his response.

"Okay. Yeah, sure, I'm okay with it," he said, then Leeza rushed at him, grabbing his stiffy.

"Guess we don't need any foreplay, as you appear to be ready to go," 'Leeza said, while pulling down his jogging pants, then ripping at her own clothes to get them off.

Chance pushed Leeza up against the wall, his fingers exploring where he could enter her. "Holy fuck, you are wet!"

"I told you it has been a while! Just get it...holy shit, Chance, fuck me, fuck me hard, fuck me harder!" Leeza screamed in between her heavy breathing and her fingernails digging into his back.

"I'm going to cum…I am going to cum…" Chance grunted as he moved quickly in and out of her. Then he held the back of her head while he whaled into her so that she wouldn't hit her head against the wall as he finished.

"That was fucking fantastic! Thank you! I so needed that," Leeza whispered as he let her down slowly.

"That was pretty great! See what you miss in the morning from guys! The morning wood!" Chance joked.

"So besides you becoming a sex maniac, what else is new with you?"

"I actually have to work tonight. I have to be there by five o'clock to get everything set up. My boss sent me home yesterday, so I told him I'd go in a little earlier today. I would've taken the day off if I knew you were coming."

"That would've defeated the surprise if I told you I was coming," Leeza chuckled. "You said your boss sent you home yesterday. Why?"

Chance looked down. "I don't want to talk about it. I'm sorry."

"It's okay. Don't worry about work, I'll just go there with you. The strip club, right?"

"Yep. The strip joint. What exactly are you going to do there? It's only all girl dancers."

Leeza looked at Chance seductively, puckering her lips. "I'm going to have fun, silly."

"What has gotten into you?" Chance asked rhetorically.

"Nothing! Literally! Three months!" Leeza said, cracking herself up, laughing loudly. "I promise I won't get in your way. I will sit peacefully in the corner."

"That grin on your face tells me otherwise."

CHAPTER 33

Lena

I had a couple more days of vacation left and knew I had to get the house ready for my best friend Becca's visit. Talk about a goofball! Becca can turn any bad situation into a good one with her sarcastic attitude. I'll admit I was always jealous of her. Her long, poker-straight brown hair and bright-green eyes could captivate just about anyone and probably anything, but even though she was drop-dead gorgeous, she never flaunted it or let it get to her head.

Becca had gone away to college after graduation while I stayed behind with my father and continued to live the country life. I didn't feel college suited me very well at the time, plus I had no clue what I wanted to do.

Grocery shopping and cleaning the house were on my to-do list before picking Becca up at the airport around five thirty this evening.

Before Bryan left for work, he told me he was going to hold off on moving the rest of his stuff in until after Becca's visit. This way he wouldn't be in the way, and Becca and I could enjoy our time together. He even let me borrow his truck to do my running around and pick Becca up from the airport.

Before leaving, I received a news update on my phone that read, "Kelly Travis, 24, from Silver Tree Acres missing since last night." It took me a minute until I realized we were in some of the same classes together in high school. Wow, wait until I tell Becca.

I spotted Becca immediately and ran her way with my arms wide open. When I reached her, I wrapped my arms around her tightly, squeezing almost all the air out of her, giving her the biggest bear hug ever.

"I've missed you so much!" I was excitedly jumping up and down.

Becca dropped her bags and began jumping up and down with me.

"It feels like it has been forever since we've seen each other!" I said, slightly exaggerating.

She kissed me on my cheek before squealing out, "I'm so excited to be here! I have so much to tell you!"

"Me too!" I said, looking down at my feet, then looking up at her slowly, kicking my one foot slowly like I was kicking dirt around, with my hands behind my back like I was embarrassed about something, although I wasn't.

"Well, let's go, girl!" Becca cheered. "We only have three days. Let's see how much trouble we can get into in three days," she said with a grin on her face.

On the ride back to my house, we decided to stop and grab a bite to eat at a little diner known as the Pig Out.

As soon as they seated us in a booth, Becca grabbed my hands.

"Guess what?" she asked excitedly.

Before I could even get the word *what* out from my mouth, she practically yelled, "I am engaged!"

I looked down and saw a gorgeous princess-cut ring sparkling on her left ring finger.

"Wow!" I said. "It's gorgeous! Congratulations, Becca, I'm so happy for you. I take it the lucky man is Kevin?"

"Of course, silly girl!" Becca said with a twitch of the hand as if she was shooing a fly away. "It happened a couple of weeks ago, but I really wanted to tell you in person. I hope you're not mad at me for not telling you sooner."

"Becca, I could never be mad at you. I'm so happy for you! You're going to get married, and to Kevin Bowe of all people. Becca Bowe, it flows so nicely," I said.

"The wedding is not for a couple of months, but it would be an honor to me if you'd be my maid of honor in the wedding. What do you say?" Becca asked, my hands still in hers.

"It would be my pleasure," I said in a sexy, serious tone. Sometimes, I must act goofy during a serious situation just to take some of the anxiety away. Both of us stood up with tears in our eyes and gave each other a nice big hug.

"Okay, so enough about me for now. Lena, what's new with you? Any men in your life that I should know about?"

"Um, no, not really. Bryan and I've been hanging out a lot lately."

"Well, that's not anything new. The two of you've been attached at the hip since, well, since your mother's wake. You two are best buddies."

"Yeah, best buddies with benefits, that is…recently," I said, looking at the table, not sure what Becca's reaction was going to be.

"Shut the fuck up! You slept with him? When? How? Oh my god, Lena, tell me you two are not like boyfriend and girlfriend!" Becca said, waiting anxiously for the response. Before I could answer, Becca began again, "I mean you two are, like, well, brother and sister. I don't really know what to say." She sounded bewildered. "Don't get me wrong, honey, I'm not trying to be mean or make fun, but… Bryan?"

"Bryan has always been there for me since my mom died. He's kind of my knight in shining armor," I said, smiling. "He may not be the cutest or the smartest, but he treats me so good I feel like he deserves a chance." Again, I looked down at the table as though I felt kind of embarrassed by my recent decisions. *But I'm not,* my inner voice protested.

"Lena, all I am saying is, just do not settle. You can't pretend to want to be with someone just because they're nice to you or because you feel bad for them. You have to love them and want to be with them."

"But I do love Bryan—" I started to say when Becca cut in again, "Lena, you and I both know you love Bryan, just not that kind of love."

"I don't know, Becca, Bryan and I just spent an amazing couple of days together out at a cabin on the lake," I said a bit defensively.

"Did he get you drunk and then you—"

"Becca, stop!" I said, a bit agitated.

"I'm sorry," Becca said softly.

"The sex was consensual. We were having a picnic, and one thing led to another. To me, it was amazing. A little uncomfortable at first..." I started, and Becca cut me off yet again.

"Lena! Please tell me this isn't your first time!" she said with raised eyebrows.

"Yes. It was, actually, and I think I chose a really great partner to be my first."

"Wow! It sounds as though you and Bryan became really close and like you really care about him. Like, care, care. I'm so sorry if I offended you. I really didn't mean to. Bryan is a really great guy. If he is what you truly want in a guy, then I am sincerely happy for you."

Chapter 34

Kelly

"It's so great to hear from you! I don't know if you know this or not, but I had the biggest crush on you in high school. So when I heard your voice over the phone, I was like, 'Oh my god, is this really happening?' You still look just as handsome as the first time I laid eyes on you!" she squealed.

"Thanks for agreeing to hang out with me. I don't have much going on for the next couple of days, and I couldn't stop thinking about you and that beautiful curly hair of yours," he said with a big grin on his face.

"You're so sweet. I always told the other girls that you weren't an oddball and that you were just quiet. Not like all the other boys."

"I'm not sure if I should take that as a compliment?" he said, sounding confused.

"So, what, like, you don't have a car?" she said, surprised.

"I do. It's just in the shop right now. I'm sorry. If you want to wait to hang out, we can—" But before he was finished with his sentence, she cut him right off.

"Oh, no, no, it's all good. We can walk wherever, that's fine with me. As long as you are by my side, I'll do just about anything," she said, with her chin touching her chest and her eyes batting like a little schoolgirl in love.

"How about we get some ice cream?" he suggested.

"Great idea!" she said with a little giggle.

"Shoot! My wallet. It's not in my pocket."

"I can go grab my purse! It's no big deal." When she turned to run back into her apartment, he grabbed her by the wrist.

"I can't let you do that. It wouldn't be right. I asked you to go out, remember? Will you just walk with me to my place so I can grab my wallet and then we could head over to the ice cream parlor right after?" he asked.

"Sure, why not! I'd love to see where you live anyway," she said excited.

When they arrived at his front door, she hesitated before going in.

"Is everything okay?" he asked as he felt her slightly hesitate and back away.

"You live here?" she asked with a confused look on her face.

"Yes, I know, it's a bit scary looking on the outside, but it gets way better on the inside, I promise," he said, grabbing her hand and pulling her through the door.

"Wait right here. Don't move. I just have to run upstairs to grab my wallet. I'll be right back down."

She stood there frozen, taking in her surroundings. The house was not better in the inside at all. It looked like a dump. She couldn't imagine someone actually living in these conditions. Before she could even think twice about leaving, she heard him say, "I'm so sorry for this."

———

Him

"I honestly had no idea that you liked me," he said, looking at her unconscious body.

"I don't think knowing that would have changed my mind at all anyways, but it's too late now. I really appreciate you giving yourself to me. I really needed to keep myself occupied for the next couple of days. I promise we're going to have so much fun!"

He slowly peeled off her clothes, revealing her breasts. Her nipples were hard, probably from it being so cold in the house since there was no electricity or gas. After removing all her clothes, he fucked her unconscious body.

When she started to come to, she felt a tightness around her throat, her vision was blurry, and she felt something warm and wet on her face.

Once her vision was clear, she saw him standing in front of her, jerking himself off.

"Why are you doing this?" she choked out, realizing that her mouth was full of some type of liquid. When she realized that it was his cum in her mouth, she started gagging and eventually vomited all over herself and onto the plastic that was between her and the floor.

"You are a sick fuck! You know that? You are a fucking freak!" she yelled. "Everyone was right about you," she spat at him.

He grabbed her chin and made her look up at his face. "I know I'm a sick fuck, but she shouldn't be having fun without me. I love her, and she should love me. End of story!"

"Who…who should love you? I don't understand what you're talking about. Please untie me and I will help you," she whined. "We can confront this bitch together!"

"How dare you call her a bitch! You fuckin' skank!"

"I'm sorry, I am so sorry. I didn't mean to call her that. I just meant if you untie me, I can help you talk to her."

"You think I'm fucking stupid, don't you? Just like the others, they begged and begged, and guess what happened to them?"

"Let me guess…they died," she said, before trying to scream at the top of her lungs.

"Bingo," he said as he swung the axe, decapitating her.

Her body fell limp onto the plastic beneath her on the wooden floor.

CHAPTER 35

Lena

"So what are the plans for today?" Becca asked cheerfully as we got up from our seats and headed toward the front door of the Pig Out.

"Well, I was thinking tonight we could hang low at the house, then tomorrow have a girls' night out. What do you think?"

"Sounds like a plan to me!" Becca said, hopping onto the passenger seat.

As we walked toward the truck, out of the corner of my eye I thought I saw Chance drive by in an orange sedan.

"Lena!" Becca yelled, startling me. I practically jumped out of my shoes.

I apparently had been so distracted that I wasn't even paying attention to where I was walking, and I almost walked right in front of a car trying to pull into a parking spot.

"Holy shit, Lena! What the heck were you thinking? You almost just got hit by a car. Are you okay?" Becca asked in a panicked voice.

I heard her, but I couldn't help but wonder if that was really him. The tall, dark, handsome stranger with the deep voice. It couldn't be him. *Why would he be here, of all places?* I asked myself.

"Are you sure you're okay, Lena?" Becca asked with worry in her voice. "You seem very distant, almost as though you saw a ghost or something."

"I'm fine," I replied with a fake laugh. Then we hopped in Bryan's F-150 and headed toward my house.

It was about 8:00 p.m. when we finally pulled up to the front of the house. Precisely then a flash of lightning lit up the entire sky like hidden fireworks behind the clouds. Both of us jumped out of the truck and ran right up the porch stairs to the front door.

"Man, this place has not changed a bit," Becca said as she walked through the door.

"You can choose where you'd like to sleep. No one is here except for me and you," I said with a big smile on my face. It had been such a long time since I hung out with a girlfriend that I was really excited and looking forward to the next couple of days together.

After Becca and I put our PJs on, we each snuggled up into a corner of the couch and decided to watch the movie *Bridesmaids*. We laughed hysterically and cracked jokes about crazy things like what happened in the movie happening in real life while we prepared for Becca's wedding.

"How did you know Kevin was the one?" I asked.

Becca looked at me and said, "I know this sounds so cliché, but I literally would get butterflies in my stomach from the sound of his voice and when he would walk into a room. Honestly I still do! Sometimes I would stumble over my words and my legs would turn to Jell-O." Becca stared off into thin air.

"You know, when Bryan and I were up at the lake, we went to this little bar, and I accidentally spilled a drink all over the front of this guy standing at the bar, and when he spoke, he had this really deep voice that for some odd reason made my heart skip a beat. I don't know what it was about him, but I felt as though I could've melted at his feet. I've never felt like that before. It was such an invigorating feeling. Today when I was in a daze outside of the Pig Out and almost got hit by that car, I thought I saw that guy driving by, but I'm pretty sure I was just seeing things," I said, looking down. "I highly doubt I'll ever see him again."

Becca sat at the corner of the couch and stared at me with her mouth agape before saying, "So let me get this straight, you found a guy who gives you butterflies and you didn't even get his phone number? Did you at least get his name?"

"Yes, actually, I did get his name. It's Chance. But I'm never going to see him again," I said, frowning at the thought. "Plus, I still think Bryan somehow is meant to be my knight in shining armor. I don't get the warm fuzzy feeling or the butterflies in my stomach, but I do really enjoy being around him."

"Fair enough," she said, then asked, "Can we go to sleep now?"

"Absolutely," I replied. "All this darn lovey-dovey talk has made me exhausted," I said, pretending to yawn.

CHAPTER 36

Chance

As Chance prepared the bar for opening, he noticed Leeza talking to the dancers, laughing and having a good time. She sat front and center of the stage while customers began to fill in the empty seats.

It was great to see her. A familiar face. The thought of her being here made him smile. He watched Leeza as she threw her money around at the dancers or tucked singles into their G-strings.

What Chance did not expect was Leeza getting onto the stage, but she fit right in like she was one of the dancers. *She was a natural*, he thought. He felt a tad bit uncomfortable when she began taking her clothes off in front of all the strange men sitting in the crowd, but he reminded himself she didn't belong to him. They were just friends.

Next up was Bethany. He was not looking forward to seeing her after their last encounter. Chance knew the music that was played for each of the girls when they danced, and instead of Britney Spears's "Toxic" coming on, Rihanna's "Work" started to play. *Odd*, Chance thought, but went about his night.

As Chance served drinks to people at the bar, he could see Leeza walking around giving lap dances to guys.

"That girl is a keeper," Ray said, patting Chance on the shoulder as he slid by him. "Where'd you meet her?" he asked with a sly smile on his face.

"She was my fiancée's best friend, my friend too."

"Wait, did you just say fiancée?" Ray asked, shocked.

"Yeah, it's a long story I'd really rather not get into right now, though," Chance said.

"No harm done here," Ray said, holding his hands into the air. "Well, she is a great girl regardless. Let her know she can come work for me anytime." Ray started to walk back toward the crowd.

"Hey, Ray, where's Bethany? I noticed her song didn't play. Is she not here today?" Chance asked quizzically.

"You love yourself some Bethany, don't you, big guy?" Ray said, laughing.

"No, that's not what I meant. I just found it odd that she was not here, that's all."

"After that night you walked in on her in my office, she hasn't been back. I haven't heard from her in days. I hope she's okay and that she'll be back soon," Ray said with little to no concern in his voice.

Weird, Chance thought. *So a girl doesn't show up for work, doesn't call in sick for days at a time, and everyone is okay with that?* He shrugged. *What the hell do I care? She's not my problem any longer.* At the end of that thought, Chance looked up to see Leeza making out with a girl in the corner.

Leeza turned her head in Chance's direction and signaled him to come over.

He lifted his hand in the air, giving her a thumbs-up that he was all good.

As the night came to an end, Chance was washing down the bar when a fully clothed Leeza came over and plopped on one of the barstools.

"So this was a fun date," she said, smiling and swaying back and forth on the chair.

"This was not a date, at least not for me," Chance said, smiling back.

"So when I was in the back hanging with the girls, they were telling me that one of the dancers, Bethany, just stopped showing up for work one day." She paused to see his reaction. When she didn't get one, she continued, "They said you and her were a 'thing.'" Leeza said with air quotes.

"We were never a 'thing,'" Chance said back with air quotes. "Apparently she's a one-and-done girl."

"They said the night you came in and they had to escort you out of the building was the last time they heard from her," Leeza said, staring at Chance.

"I asked Ray earlier why she was not here today, and he said the same thing."

"Do you still care about her?" she asked, teasingly.

"Not at all. There was nothing to care about. Anyhoo, let's wrap up and call it a night, or should I say morning," he joked.

CHAPTER 37

Lena

Peeves was beginning to fill in. It must've been 9:00 p.m. Suddenly, I heard, "Hey, pretty lady, I think I've seen you around before. Can I get you a drink?" And there he was, standing right before me with his dark hair, light eyes, and sexy, deep voice.

"Chance, right?" I stuttered, sounding like an idiot.

"Impressive, you remembered my name! Do you come here often?"

"Not really, but I'm here today because my best friend is in town. Speaking of which, Becca, this is Chance."

"Well, hello, Chance. Love the name!" Becca said as she extended out her hand to shake his.

Then he quickly turned his head to look back at me, and while looking me up and down, he whispered, "You look really nice tonight."

I was wearing an outfit I'd bought earlier while Becca and I were out shopping. Normally I'd never dress like this, but I really wanted to feel sexy, and the little black dress I was wearing did just that. The dress had spaghetti straps that crisscrossed in the back, and the front dipped so low that my cleavage was showing. The dress came just above my knees and fit as snug as a glove. It revealed every curve of my body, and I became aware of Chance not being able to take his eyes off me, and I was honestly loving every minute of it.

When Becca and I walked away, I could feel his stare going right through me. Sir Mix-a-Lot's "Baby Got Back" started playing loudly over the speakers, and I couldn't help myself, I purposely started dancing seductively on the dance floor in an effort to keep his attention on me. When I spun away from Becca, there he was practically on top of me. We were directly face-to-face. I took my right hand, and starting from his left shoulder, I slowly slid my hand and body down his body. Then I took both of my hands and placed them on each side of his body as I made my way back up.

At this point, I had several drinks in me, but it didn't stop me from allowing him to do what he did next. When our eyes met, he cupped my face with both of his hands and pulled me closer to his, then kissed my top lip gently and softly bit my bottom lip before he began to kiss me hard and vigorously.

When Chance moved from kissing my lips to kissing my neck, when I opened my eyes, we were suddenly no longer at Peeves. We were in a room I didn't recognize, but I was so consumed in the moment that I didn't even care where I was.

Chance slid his hand up my leg until he reached the bottom of my dress, then he slowly lifted my dress up until he completely removed it from my body. I stood in front of him in just my black lace strapless bra with matching panties, breathing heavy, feeling high on life because I wanted this man to take me. All of me.

His soft tongue licked my neck and then worked its way to my breasts. He didn't go under or remove my bra. He just licked the skin that was showing. Then his tongue made its way from my breasts to my belly button. The warm, wet feeling of his tongue gliding down my body made me moist, extremely moist, between my legs, and as his tongue made its way to my inner thighs, I lost all control, and it felt like a jolt of electricity just shot through my body.

My eyes shot open as my body was involuntarily trembling from a wonderful sensation I'd never felt in my entire life. I looked around and realized I was all alone in my bed, in my house, with wet underwear, from a dream.

Holy shit, I think I just had my first real orgasm!

CHAPTER 38

Lena

Becca woke up to the aroma of bacon and eggs. She followed the mouthwatering smell down the stairs and toward the kitchen.

I had the table all set up and the food served hot and ready to eat. I dished out the last hash brown just as Becca walked into the kitchen.

"Wow, look at all this food! It's only eight fifteen, what the heck time did you get up to prepare all of this?" she asked in astonishment, still rubbing the crusties from her eyes.

I couldn't help but laugh because of the look on her face and at the thought of why I was up so early. "I got up at seven thirty. I had an interesting awakening, and I was so worked up that I couldn't fall back to sleep, so I decided to make myself useful."

"Worked up, huh?" Becca said, eyeing me with one eyebrow raised.

"Don't laugh," I began. "I had this amazing, mind-boggling dream about that guy Chance, the one I told you about from the bar, deep voice. Well, anyway, while I was dreaming, my body began to tremble violently, and there was this tingling sensation. I think I may have actually—" Before I could finish what I was saying, Becca cut me off, almost spitting her orange juice in the air, yelling, "What! No way! You lucky little bitch! No wonder the smile has not left your face this morning."

I could feel my face turn bright red.

"How about we go shopping this afternoon to find outfits to wear this evening?" Becca suggested with excitement in her eyes.

"Sounds like fun to me!"

While Becca was in the shower, she yelled out, "While we're out, can we try on some bridesmaid dresses?"

"Sure!" I agreed, although I wasn't too keen on the idea, but knew it had to get done.

———

We hopped into the F-150. "I can't believe Bryan let you use his truck to hang out with me," Becca said.

"He loves me...and trusts me," I gloated.

We spent about seven hours trying on bridesmaid dresses, wedding gowns, and night-out clothes. It was a pretty successful day. I found a beautiful purple sparkling strapless bridesmaid dress, and Becca found a gorgeous wedding gown. We even found the flowers she wanted in her bouquet, and we also were successful in finding outfits to wear for our girls' night out. We were extremely giddy from the excitement of shopping.

Before getting ready for the night, we grabbed a glass of wine, plopped down on the couch, and turned on the old boob tube to see what the weather was going to be like for the evening.

Just as we were about to turn off the television, "Breaking News" flashed across the screen, so we waited to see what it was about. As we sat there watching, a picture of Kelly Travis, a girl we went to high school with, was showing, and we could not believe the words coming out of the telecaster's mouth. Kelly's decapitated head was found twenty feet from her dismembered body. We sat there in silence with our mouths agape.

"So that was not the best way to start our night out," Becca said, breaking the silence.

"I can't believe she was murdered. Not like I was great friends with her or anything," I said, turning off the TV, "but friends or not, I feel terrible. I am pretty sure she had a huge crush on Bryan when we were in school."

"No way!" Becca shot back.

"Yep! I wonder if Bryan saw the news."

"The news is very sad," she said, "but I don't think we cancel our plans."

"Yeah, you're right," I agreed. "We did just buy these awesome outfits."

Becca walked out of the spare bedroom into the hallway in her new jean skirt, a white off-the-shoulder fitted top, and white wedges that had flowers on them. Her silky brown hair was in big beautiful curls that hung down her back. I stood there in awe. I was wearing my new white jean skirt with a black sleeveless triangle top, paired with black strapless heels. My hair was in a side pony that sat on my shoulder with blond cascading curls. We smiled at each other then went arm in arm down the stairs. God, I had missed my best friend. We decided on one more glass of wine before heading out. Our goal was to loosen up prior to going out. This way we'd be ready to dance.

I knew Becca loved to dance, and she would kind of lose her temper a bit if you tried to stop and sit down. Therefore, I had to make sure I was ready and had my dancing shoes on.

CHAPTER 39

Bethany

"How's it hanging?" he asked, laughing.

"Sometimes I really crack myself up. Do you get it? How's it hanging? I bet if you could actually talk right now, you'd say, 'I'm not hanging so good.' Hey, at least I'm in a good mood, at least for the moment. That's until I start thinking about the fact that I would be with Lena right now if it were not for Becca being here. You're probably thinking, 'Why did I get into your car the other night?' That honestly was a really stupid mistake on your part. You're just a stripper, though, so it's not like anyone is going to miss you. Just one less whore on the street giving her body up for cash."

Bethany could barely keep her eyes open.

She was weak.

Very weak.

She couldn't yell at him because he had so generously cut her tongue out days earlier. He'd wrapped what was left of her tongue in a bunch of gauze to keep her from bleeding out. He needed to keep her alive because he needed someone to take his anger out on. Why not a useless stripper who means absolutely nothing to him?

"You are looking a little pale. Here, let me grab the stool so you can stand on it and rest your arms a little while," he offered as he lifted her up to place the stool under her feet.

However, Bethany was so weak she could not hold herself up. Her wrists were raw from the rope rubbing against them for days. Her skin was so pale that almost every vein in her body was visible.

"I know you're probably hoping that someone walks in to save you, but I hate to tell you this, no one comes inside this barn anymore. Except for me, that is."

He sat down on the stool next to Bethany's almost-lifeless body, having a conversation with her as if they were just two good friends hanging out.

"The suffering will end soon, I promise," he said while looking down at his hands. "You did last a lot longer than I honestly thought you would. You look like shit, by the way. You're all pale like Casper the Friendly Ghost. I really do love the woman, don't get me wrong, but sometimes she just makes me so mad that I want to hit her, but I can't, so I take it out on other women…like yourself.

"I wonder what she's doing right now. I fell in love with Lena the moment I saw her. Blond hair like the sand, blue eyes like the ocean, and a bangin' body. She's the one, I tell ya, there's no doubt in my mind. She'll be my wife someday. You certainly don't have much to say," he said, looking up at Bethany, who just stared straight at the ground.

"I don't understand why you look so sad. Just think, you get to go to heaven soon and be with the Almighty Lord. It'll be a way better life up there for you. You're nothing down here but a piece of garbage. Just think, you'll soon be a beautiful angel with wings. I bet you'll have a ton of friends, unlike down here. People only talk to you because they know you'll give it up easily. Do you have sex with women too? I didn't think you would answer that question, but I just had to ask.

"I never look at other girls like I do Lena. She's special. So don't think for one second you are better than her. I'm only here because she wanted to go out with her friend, and I didn't want to be alone. Maybe I should go surprise her. Then again, maybe she'll get mad, and I don't want her to be mad. I can wait. I've waited this long."

CHAPTER 40

Lena

On our drive to the bar, I thought I saw Chance drive right past us. I tried speeding up, but there were cars in front of us, so I didn't get very far. I began to wonder if Chance was staying here in town or maybe he just had a look-alike. With that last thought, Becca and I pulled into the parking lot at good ol' Peeves.

"Wow, this place is packed," Becca said, smiling.

Almost every table was taken. "You go grab a table, and I'll go grab the first round," I said excited.

Although Becca was about to get married, she still felt a need to flirt, or at least think she still could, so she chose to sit next to a table that a bunch of guys occupied. She looked their way and gave them her flirty little smile and wave.

"Um, what're you up to, missy?" I said jokingly to Becca with a questioning look upon my face.

"Hey, I can still look all I want. I just can't touch!" she said with a huge smile on her face. "It's strictly just harmless flirting!"

After three hours and a bunch of shots, we were feeling pretty good. Ginuwine's "My Pony" started blaring over the speakers, so Becca and I immediately ran to the dance floor. We began swinging our hips and grinding up on each other, and the men in the bar were yelling and whistling at us, cheering us on. I must admit, we were both loving all the attention we were receiving. The more the crowd cheered, the more Becca and I got into it. We became so in the moment of dancing, next thing we knew, we were climbing on top of the bar and continued to dance up there. One of the girls tending bar

114

handed both Becca and I a bottle of cherry-flavored vodka and asked if we would give shots out to the crowd.

Becca and I went to different ends of the bar and began pouring shots of vodka into each giddy customer's mouth. When I was about six people in, as I was pouring a shot into a guy's mouth, I immediately recognized the eyes. I felt as though my entire body went numb. A moment later, I realized I was still pouring the cherry vodka into his mouth, and it was overflowing out of his mouth and down his neck.

"Oh my god! Oh my god! I am so sorry! Really! I really am so sorry!" I said, trembling. I couldn't believe he was actually here. He was really here, right in front of me, at the local bar in my hometown.

As I continued to pour shots into the mouths of the very happy-drunk strangers, I began to feel hot and flushed, and my legs began to feel like jelly. I wondered how long he had been here. *Oh jeez, did he see me dancing on the bar? What an idiot!* I scolded myself. *Hopefully he doesn't think I do this all the time. Wait! Why do I care what he thinks? I don't even know this guy!* Out of curiosity, I turned to look back down the bar to see if he was still there, and to my disappointment, he was gone.

I couldn't believe that I once again spilled alcohol on him, only this time I almost drowned him in it! *I am such a ditz!*

After Becca and I got down from the bar, I looked around to see if he happened to still be here. My heart skipped a beat when I noticed him sitting in a corner, just like before, only this time he was accompanied by a beautiful woman with long black hair. I couldn't help but notice what a gorgeous smile he had and how happy he looked.

"Lena, h-e-l-l-o? What are you, or should I say who are you, staring at?" Becca asked with a rhythmic tone in her voice.

"What? Who? What do you mean?" I stuttered.

"Really, Captain Obvious? Do I really have to spell it out for you?" Becca asked with her head tilted to the one side waiting for an answer from me, her best friend.

"Okay, okay, let's sit down and do not look over there for at least a good ten minutes after I tell you, agreed?" I pressed.

"I agree," Becca said, holding up her pinky finger.

"Remember that dreamy guy I was telling you about, with the deep voice and the telling eyes? Well, he is here…in the corner… with that gorgeous black-haired woman. Don't look now, though. Seriously do not look, I mean it! Bec—"

Before I could even finish my sentence, Becca looked. She couldn't resist, and I could tell she spotted him right away as well as the gorgeous black-haired woman he was with.

"I love you, darling," Becca said as sweetly as she possibly could. "Unfortunately, you have nothing on her. I mean that in the nicest way possible. Lena, I love you, but she is drop-dead gorgeous. Which makes me wonder what they're doing here in this neck of the woods. They totally do not fit in a place like this."

Every time I glanced over at Chance, he was looking my way even though that beautiful creature was sitting right in front of him.

"Wow! He looks like he has some junk in his trunk," Becca said in a drunken stupor.

"Really, Becca! Binoculars? Who in their right mind carries binoculars with them in their purse? Are you trying to embarrass me?" I asked.

"Whoops! I think he may've caught me looking at his crotch. Oh, boy, he is getting up!" Becca said with a bit of excitement in her voice. "I think I need to use the ladies' room," Becca said running off.

"Lena, right?" the deep, sexy voice asked.

I quickly turned to meet the most gorgeous green eyes, perfect lips. "Yes, that's correct. You got me." *"You got me." Who says that? I must've sounded so stupid!*

"Forgive me if my eyes failed me, but did your friend just have binoculars?" Chance asked.

"Um, I'm not sure," I said, trying to play dumb.

"Hi there! I am Becca, Lena's best friend," Becca said in a flirty voice, extending her hand toward Chance.

Taking Becca's hand and kissing it, Chance replied, "Hi, Becca, I'm Chance. Nice to meet you. Hey, were you by any means just holding up bino—" Chance didn't get to finish his sentence before he was distracted by the black-haired beauty waving him down.

"Excuse me, ladies," he said politely. "I must go, I'm being summoned, but it was really nice to meet you, Becca, and very good to see you, Lena. Hope I'll see you ladies around town." He winked as he walked away.

"Wow, Lena! He's a real hottie! Now I know why you're having wild dreams at night," Becca said, moving her eyebrows up and down.

"Ha-ha! Very funny!" I mocked. "Enough about him, let's get some more shots!" I yelled, holding my beer up in the air.

I was trying very hard to distract myself, but it wasn't working very well. My heart was still racing, and I really wanted to look back toward the corner so bad just to have another look at him and those piercing green eyes. I really couldn't understand why I felt this way when he was around, and I couldn't help but wonder who the girl was that he was with. She didn't look familiar, and sadly, when you live in a small town, you pretty much know everybody! I think I was actually feeling jealous, but I'm not sure why. *It isn't like I knew this man*, I thought, trying to convince myself. *Well, I mean, I did spill alcohol on him twice, but hell, we've never had a serious conversation.*

"Here you go, girl! We're getting trashed tonight!" Becca tried yelling over the music.

"Cheers to girls' night out!" I screamed as we clinked our shot glasses together.

After swallowing my shot, I looked around to see if I could spot Chance. He was nowhere in sight. *Oh, poop, he must've left.* My excitement slowly started to fade away, and disappointment began to set in again.

What's it about this man that I can't seem to shake? Then another shot.

CHAPTER 41

Lena

"Lena, hon, are you okay in there? You've been in there for three and half hours now. You can't possibly have any more to throw up. Would you like me to get you something?" Becca asked, tapping on the bathroom door.

I slowly crawled over to the door and opened it a crack. It felt like the biggest challenge I ever had to do. Every single part of my body ached. I peeked out at Becca as I was kneeling on the floor with one hand and the other hand on the doorknob. It took so much effort to try and balance myself.

I looked at Becca and said, very slowly and drawn out, "I. Am. Never. Ever. Drinking again."

———

Bryan

"Hey, babe! How are you feeling? You look like you had a really good time last night."

My head quickly snapped up. "Bryan? What're you doing here?"

"Becca called me to let me know you weren't feeling well. She was concerned after three hours passed and you still didn't come out of the bathroom. Plus, she needs a ride to the airport and didn't think you were in any shape to drive her," Bryan said matter-of-factly.

"Thanks, Becca. Thanks, Bryan," I said drearily as I slowly laid back down on the cold bathroom floor. Not even a minute passed before I raced back to the toilet, which apparently was going to be my new BFF for the day.

Bryan came into the bathroom and held my hair then quietly asked if I needed anything before taking Becca to the airport. All I could do was slowly shake my head no before laying my head on my arm, which was resting on the toilet seat.

Bryan left for a second and returned with a hair tie. He pulled my hair away from my face and put it in a ponytail. Then he grabbed a washcloth, ran it under cold water, and placed it on the back of my neck, which felt extremely cold at first, but then felt really good. When he walked out of the bathroom, I figured he was off to take Becca to the airport, then he popped back in to give me a glass of ice water and two Tylenol. *Why was he so damn sweet?* He gently kissed my cheek, and then off he went with Becca.

"So you girls had a pretty eventful night, I take it?" Bryan said, smirking at Becca in his passenger seat.

"Yes, apparently too much fun. We had a few too many shots!" Becca said, giggling. "At one point I had to bring Lena back to earth after she spotted this really hot guy that she ran into not that long ago, and I think she was kind of jealous." Becca looked at Bryan to see what his reaction was.

He stared straight ahead, but then he asked, "Why would you say that? Why would she be jealous?"

Having fun, messing with Bryan, knowing that he cared about Lena, she answered, "Because he was with this black-haired beauty with green eyes."

"Oh" was all that escaped from Bryan's mouth. But she could tell by his body language that he was agitated.

"So Lena told me the two of you are going to be roommates soon," Becca said, still looking at Bryan.

"Yep. That is the rumor flying around."

"Well, I hope things work out for the two of you. I love you both, but of course I love her more, so you know I'll always take her side. You better be good to her and treat her with respect," Becca said in a scolding, but jokingly, manner.

"Whoa, whoa, slow down there, chicka. You act like we're getting married," Bryan said, but also thinking to himself that would be the greatest thing to happen in his life. No one, not even him, understood why he craved her so much. "We're only moving in together," he replied kind of defensively.

"I know," Becca said, "I'm just messing with you, sort of. Don't get your panties in a bunch. All I'm saying is she is sensitive, and she knows absolutely nothing about relationships. All she really knows is, well, you."

"Again, we're not getting married," Bryan replied, again a bit defensively. "And that's not a bad thing that I'm all she knows."

"I know," Becca agreed. "I just worry about her, that's all."

Bryan looked over at Becca at first with a look of anger but then calmly said, "That's understandable. You are of course her one and only best friend," Bryan said, sounding a bit sarcastic.

Inside he was raging.

"Well, here's your stop, Becca. I truly hope you ladies had a good time. I'm sure I'll be seeing you around again," Bryan said as Becca jumped out of the truck.

She looked back in at Bryan and said, "Oh, you will! And sooner than you think!" She chuckled, then followed up with, "Lena will fill you in once she is feeling better. Goodbye, handsome, it was great to see you again. Thank you so much for letting us use your truck to get around town, and thank you for the ride to the airport!" Becca said. "Oh! Don't forget what I said about being good to her. If you're not good to her, I'll hunt you down and kill you! That's a promise!" With that, Becca gently closed his truck door and headed toward the automatic doors that welcome you into the airport.

On the ride back to Lena's house, Bryan couldn't help but wonder about this Chance guy. *Why does he keep showing up places? And why does Lena seem to have an attraction to him?* The thought made Bryan's stomach turn. He tried hard to shake the thought.

CHAPTER 42

Bryan

Bryan put all the negative thoughts aside and focused on his excitement about moving in with Lena today. As Bryan jumped out of his truck, he realized Lena might still be sick. He ran up the front porch stairs and as he entered the house yelled, "Lena, are you okay up there?" Bryan's heart skipped a beat as he thought the worst when he received no response, but he almost burst into tears of laughter when he opened the bathroom door to find Lena sprawled out on the floor sound asleep with the wet washcloth covering her eyes. Instead of waking her, he decided to join her by lying down next to her on the bathroom floor.

―――――

Lena

When I woke up, the sun was starting to set. I looked over to see Bryan lying next to me, just opening his eyes.

"Holy cow. I can't believe I slept that good and that long on a bathroom floor of all places," I said, shocked.

"Me either," Bryan agreed, turning on his side and propping his head up on one hand looking directly at me.

"Oh my gosh!" I yelled a little too loud, scaring us both.

"What? What is it?" Bryan asked, looking around the bathroom as if they were not alone.

"We were supposed to move you in today. I'm so sorry," I said with a sad look on my face, placing my head into my hands.

"No worries, babe. We still have tomorrow. Or the next day. Or the day after that," Bryan said sarcastically. "I'm just glad that you're feeling better," he said while gently lifting my face with his hands.

"I know the bathroom floor is clean because I just cleaned it myself. However, I still find it a weee bit disgusting that we just slept on it," I said, looking at Bryan and laughing.

"Well, technically you were on the floor. I was actually on the rug," Bryan teased.

I closed my eyes and stuck my tongue out at him.

"Okay, why don't you shower, and I'll go cook us some dinner," Bryan suggested.

"Absolutely," I agreed with a huge smile on my face.

When I stepped out of the shower, the smell of steak immediately permeated my nostrils. *This whole moving-in-together thing may have some great benefits to it,* I thought.

While I was getting dressed, my stomach growled loudly at me as I inhaled the yummy smell of food that I'd deprived myself of all day long. Stupid hangover!

Running down the stairs into the dining room, I stopped dead in my tracks as I couldn't believe my eyes. Rose petals covered the dining room table, as well as the floor. Candles were lit. A bouquet of roses sat in the very center of the table. Dinner was also on the table, and Bryan was standing next to a chair waiting to pull it out for me. What a gentleman.

"Bryan, I can't believe you did all of this!" I said with pure shock in my voice.

"Just say you will—" Bryan began, but stupid me jumped up out of my seat, startling him.

"Will what? Whoa!" I said accusingly.

"Sit back down, goofball. You didn't even let me finish my sentence," Bryan said, holding his hands in the air. "I was saying, before you jumped to conclusions, just say you will eat all of this delicious food I made for you. You're going to need all the energy you can get to help me move my shit over here!" he said, laughing. "Jeez, what'd you think, I was going to ask you to marry me?" Bryan asked rhetorically. "Now shall we eat this feast I have prepared?"

———

It was almost eleven thirty when we decided this would be the last load we would be moving for the evening.

"Let's have a couple of beers and watch *Nightmare on Elm Street*, Bryan suggested as his eyes lit up.

"I'm all about the movie, but I'm definitely going to pass on the beer. How about some Kool-Aid?" I asked.

"Sure thing," Bryan said happily. "Hey, before we get into anything, what was Becca referring to when she said you'd fill me in on something?"

"Oh my goodness, I forgot to tell you. Becca's getting married!" I said excitedly, clapping my hands and bouncing up and down like a little kid on Christmas. "Do you want to be my date?" I asked Bryan, batting my eyes and tilting my head.

"Now how could I possibly say no to those puppy-dog eyes?" Bryan said, making a pouty face.

"Okay now, let's see who can get their jammies on first," I challenged. Both of us darted up the stairs. Three minutes later, we both came running out of our bedrooms. Me in my tank top and shorts, Bryan in his boxer briefs. I quickly jumped in front of Bryan, blocking him from getting to the stairs.

"Whoa, whoa, whoa, what makes you think those are sleepwear attire?" I asked, looking down at Bryan's navy-blue-checkered boxer briefs.

"You're joking, right?" Bryan asked, staring at me. "He's covered!"

"Can't you just put on a pair of shorts or flannel pants?" I asked, blushing.

"If it's really making you that uncomfortable," Bryan said, sounding disappointed.

"No. You know what, this is your house too now. You can wear whatever you please. I'm not being fair. I'm sorry." As I was apologizing, Bryan ran past me and yelled "Beat you!" from the bottom of the stairs.

"This is war, mister!" I yelled back, running down the stairs.

Bryan ran and dove onto the couch, and then I followed right behind. After I landed on Bryan's back, we bounced off the couch and landed together on the floor. We were laughing so hard I almost peed my pants.

"Okay, now go get my Kool-Aid, cheater! I'll put the movie in."

"Sure," Bryan replied walking away.

A few minutes later, I yelled, "Movie is about to start! What's taking so long?"

"Because you never mentioned that I needed to make the Kool-Aid first!" he yelled back.

When Bryan came back into the living room, I suggested we turn out the lights to make it spookier. The next thing I knew, the sun was shining brightly over my eyelids, and I woke up to something poking me directly in the center of my lower back. When I finally opened my eyes, I realized I wasn't in my bedroom, which meant I slept on the couch, which also meant there was a good possibility Bryan also fell asleep on the couch. Which then led me to believe that the thing poking me in my back was most likely not a spring from the couch.

I gently slid myself forward and off the couch hoping to not to wake him. I wasn't going to, but I couldn't resist—I had to look at what had been poking me. I put my hands to my mouth as I gasped the words "Oh my god." I quickly turned away, blushing like a little schoolgirl who just saw something she shouldn't have.

All I could think about when I showered was, *What a great way to start a morning!*

CHAPTER 43

Lena

"Good morning!" I said as I sat down at the kitchen table to eat breakfast.

"Good morning to you, li'l lady! Why are you so smiley this morning?" Bryan asked as he gently laid scrambled eggs and three pieces of sausage onto the plate in front of me.

"Do I really have to have a reason to be smiley and happy?" I asked while taking my first bite of the eggs.

"Nope. Not at all. I definitely can get used to this," Bryan mumbled to himself.

"Hey, what do you say we go shopping for a tux for you for Becca's wedding when we get out of work today? I could look for some new shoes."

At first Bryan didn't look too thrilled, but then he surprised me.

"Sure! We can catch some dinner after if you'd like," Bryan suggested.

"Awesome! Let's take the truck to work this morning. This way we can get into town a little faster and have more time to shop," I proposed. With that, we wrapped up breakfast, headed out to the truck, and off to work we went.

When we arrived at Frederick's, I hopped out of the truck, and as I was closing the door, Bryan yelled, "See you at five o'clock sharp!" and drove off to Constantine's.

Chance

"You should really consider getting a new car before this one takes its last breath and dies," Leeza said jokingly, looking at Chance.

"You kind of need money to get a new car, and I'm definitely nowhere near having that kind of money. I came here with very little and had to use it for housing, food, and some new clothes. So unfortunately, this rusty old sedan needs to keep kicking a little, I mean a lot, longer. Bartending is not the best-paying job, but it's a start," Chance said, looking back at Leeza.

"Are you sure you're going to be okay here? I mean, Silver Tree Acres is a nice place, but it's kind of homely. It's probably safe for you to come back home now. Are you sure you don't want to come back?" Leeza pleaded.

"Leeza, this is my home now. I'm happy here. It's a different pace, but I like it," Chance said with a smile.

"Well, okay then. Promise me if you need anything at all or just want to talk, you'll call me." Leeza waited for a response, and since it didn't come fast enough, she blurted "Promise me!" loudly, scaring a little old lady walking past the car.

"Nice job!" Chance said jokingly. "I promise I'll call."

"Even if it's just a 'friends with benefits' call, you better call," she said teasingly.

On the drive back to his apartment, Chance wondered if the hot blonde frequented Peeves often. He laughed to himself when he thought about the startled look on the beauty's face when she noticed him, while almost drowning him.

Thinking about her actually turned him on.

When he got back to his apartment, he grabbed his phone, went to his videos, and pressed play. There she was. Dancing on the bar, in that sexy outfit. He had secretly recorded her at the bar, not a long recording, but just enough that he could see her and watch her dance for him repeatedly—well, at least in his mind she was dancing for him.

Chance watched the video in slow motion until he could not take it anymore. He went and grabbed the baby oil and put it on himself so it would be easier to masturbate. He closed his eyes and envisioned her naked on the bar. A couple seconds later, he ejaculated into a towel that was laying nearby.

For a second, he thought about Amanda and felt guilty. Then he began crying into his hands.

"What the fuck's happening to me right now?" Chance asked out loud, knowing that no one was going to answer him.

Since he had to work at Wesley's tonight, he decided he was going to take a shower now and sneak in a nap.

While showering, his thoughts flipped back and forth from Amanda to Lena.

CHAPTER 44

Lena

"Seriously, Bryan? I wouldn't have even suggested doing this had I known how picky you were with clothing," I grumbled.

"Hey! This isn't just any piece of clothing here. We're talking about a tuxedo!" Bryan said, trying to keep a straight face. "Usually, I really don't care about what I'm wearing, but since I am going to be courting the hottest woman around town, I need to look at least somewhat worthy."

"Okay, that's fine and all, but you've tried on thirteen different tuxedos! Thirteen!" I emphasized. "And I honestly hate to say this, but they all look the same to me, but if I had to choose one, it would be the third one you tried on. The gray one with the silky white vest and black tie. You looked really sexy in that one," I said, making a purring sound.

"Really?" Bryan asked in a high-pitched voice, which made us both laugh hysterically.

"Seriously, though, I do really like that one. Can we please get it so that we can go get something to eat? I am starving!" I whined.

Once Bryan agreed, I clasped my hands together in a gesture as if I was praying, whispering, "Thank you, thank you, thank you."

The restaurant we chose to go to, Clarissa's, was within the mall. Very high end. The lighting was dim, and there were lit candles on each and every one of the tables, which set the ambience. The one wall was decorated with a brass waterfall, which gave the place a very serene feeling.

"Hey, Mr. High Roller, you sure you can afford this?" I teased, looking around taking the scenery in.

"Ouch!" Bryan said, holding his right hand to his heart. "Do you really think I'm that cheap?" he asked with disappointment in his voice. "Maybe I choose to save my money for bigger and better things, maybe even shinier things."

That shut me up quickly, took the smile right from my face. Oh boy, now my mind was wandering. What did he mean by shinier things? Just as I was about to go into a full-blown panic attack, the waiter showed up to take our order. We both ordered steak dinners.

"So when you say shinier things, are you talking about jewelry or, like, a car?" I asked, probing.

Ignoring my question, Bryan changed the subject. "What do you think about taking a walk along the beach after dinner? It's such a nice night out."

"I think you just totally changed the subject on purpose," I said, pouting.

"What? Me? No. I don't know what you're talking about," Bryan said sarcastically. "Oh my, look at that, our food is coming. Does a walk sound good?" he pressed.

"Sure, why not," I said shrugging my shoulders.

After we finished dinner, we took a drive down to the place everyone called Ghetto Beach. I removed my shoes before getting out of the truck. Bryan extended his hand to help me out of the truck, and he continued to hold my hand as we made our way down to the beach. The sand squished between my toes. It was such a great evening. Very romantic. Yet I couldn't get this queasy feeling out of my stomach. All that talk about shiny things at dinner really got my mind racing, and I wasn't really sure what to expect from this walk on the beach.

"Isn't this a perfect night for a walk on the beach?" Bryan asked, turning and looking at me.

"Yes, yes, it is" I stammered.

"Are you okay? You seem kind of nervous or something. Are you feeling all right?" Bryan asked with concern in his voice, placing both of his hands on my shoulders.

"Oh, no, I'm fine. There's nothing wrong," I lied.

"Lena, do you want to just go home? We can take a walk on the beach some other time," Bryan offered.

"Really?" I said, a bit too excitedly.

"Really," Bryan said, looking at me quizzically.

"So you were not planning on popping the question?"

With a stunned look on his face, he said, "Oh my goodness, Lena. No. We literally just moved in together. We are roommates, best friends. I know that, why would I...no, of course not."

I couldn't read Bryan's face, but still I took a deep breath and replied "Oh, good. I was a little worried at dinner with the talk about shiny things, and then a romantic walk on the beach, I honestly thought you had something up your sleeve," I said with a sigh of relief.

"Now just for thinking that...tickle tackle!" Bryan yelled, and down we went into the sand, laughing and rolling around.

Bryan was on top looking down at me and said, "I can't believe you actually thought I was going to ask you to marry me, you silly girl."

In a way, Bryan felt sad thinking about what if he did ask her. Would she have said no? Would she have kicked me out? Bryan decided to scratch the nasty thoughts and focused rather on making Lena laugh and enjoying the moment.

An unexpected flash of lightning lit up the sky, followed by a loud crash of thunder that made us both scream. Then we looked at each other, laughing at our reaction. Before we reached the truck, we got stuck in a torrential downpour. Once we were in the truck, which was only a couple seconds later, we were drenched from head to toe.

CHAPTER 45

Chance

"Chance, my boy!" Ray yelled from across the room. "Come and meet Janea! Janea is going to be Bethany's replacement, as I am pretty sure she is not coming back. Janea, this is our handsome bartender, Chance," Ray said, looking back and forth from Chance then to Janea.

"Go on, toots, go get ready," Ray said, slapping Janea on her right ass cheek.

'She's a pretty one, now, isn't she, big boy?" Ray said with a no-good smirk on his face.

"She is very pretty," Chance replied. "Now don't you go getting any crazy ideas in your head, Ray. I can see it by the look in your eye that you are up to no good," Chance said while he wiped down the countertop.

"Well, in case you're interested, she's single." Ray winked and walked away.

Just as the first girl was about to step onto stage, all the lights in the place went out. The music screeched to a halt, and Chance could hear loud crashes of thunder outside.

After waiting for about a half an hour, when the power still had not come on, Ray decided to ask the crowd if they wanted to stick around, saying they could rig up a way to have light on the stage and play music from their phones. The crowd agreed, whistling and clapping loudly.

Ray, Chance, and DJ Kool used rope to hang some flashlights over the stage. DJ Kool quickly put together a playlist for the girls, and although the music was not amplified, they made it work.

With the light from his phone, Chance was able to put drinks together at the bar.

After dancing, the new girl, Janea, came over to the bar and ordered a drink.

"Can I please get a Stoli and cran?" she asked.

"Absolutely, for a pretty girl like you," Chance said, smiling.

"Hey, could you possibly walk with me to the changing room so I can see where I am going? My phone is in the locker in the back."

Janea had that young-girl cuteness to her, and she had such a sweet, innocent voice.

As Chance and Janea entered the back room, Janea grabbed his phone and ran off.

"Janea? Janea? Where'd you go? Janea? Are you okay? Can you hear me?" Chance began to panic, thinking the worst.

A few seconds later, he heard a whisper, "Chance, come over here."

"How can I come to you if I can't see anything?" Chance asked, still nervous.

"Just follow my voice."

As Chance rounded the corner of the changing room, he felt a hand grab his crotch. He jumped from the scare, but then decided to go along with it. *What the hell,* he thought.

She was seated on a bench and pulled him closer to her. She unzipped his pants and maneuvered his penis out. Then he felt her mouth moving up and down and her tongue in a circular motion from the bottom to the top. Almost climaxing, he grabbed her head and pulled her up so that they were face-to-face, then he swiftly turned her around against the lockers and fucked the shit out of her from behind.

As they were getting dressed, the lights came back on. He looked over to Janea, and she wasn't smiling. Instead she had tears in her eyes.

"Hey, whoa, are you okay?" Chance asked, concerned.

"Yeah, I'm fine," she whispered.

"Then why are you crying? Did I hurt you? I'm—"

Before Chance could finish his sentence, she cut him off. "No. You didn't do anything wrong. I was instructed to give you pleasure," Janea said, looking down.

"You were instructed? By whom?"

"The owner."

"Ray? No, Ray would never do that," Chance said accusingly.

"Okay," Janea agreed.

"Okay? What's okay? I feel like a terrible person. Why would Ray send you to do something like that?" Chance asked, sounding confused.

"He said I had to earn my keep, so he told me to pick someone, and I chose you," she said, now with tears slowly dripping down her face.

Chance got down on his knees to her level and apologized profusely. "Please accept my apology. I'll have a talk with Ray. Why don't you finish getting dressed and go home for the evening? I'll tell him you were not feeling well."

Janea nodded in agreement but kept her head down. After she finished getting dressed, she walked toward the back door, but before she left, she turned one more time to look at Chance, only she was no longer Janea. She was Amanda. "I love you, Chance."

As Chance went to follow her, the minute he touched the back door, sirens went off.

"What the, oh my god, are you serious?" he said out loud, looking over at his alarm clock. He realized that he had been dreaming, and the sirens he heard were his alarm going off. *You have got to be kidding me,* he thought. *It was so real. She was so real. Why did Amanda appear? Was my dream trying to tell me something? That's foolish,* he thought as he rolled out of bed to get ready for work.

It's called guilt, Chance told himself. *Now if I walk into work and there really is a new girl named Janea, I'll freak the fuck out. This shit is crazy. Am I losing it? I'm still too young to be losing it, right? Well, then again, I'm having a conversation in my head with myself.*

On that note, I'm having a shot, and off to work I shall go.

CHAPTER 46

Lena

On the drive home, I couldn't help but keep glancing over at Bryan. He was all wet from the downpour, and the look kind of turned me on. There was something about the way the water dripped slowly from his hair onto his cheek down to his lips. *Whoa! What am I doing?*

When I wasn't looking at him, I could feel him looking at me. I could feel that my nipples were hard from the cold rain that soaked my shirt, and the more I thought about him looking at them, the harder they got.

As soon as Bryan put the truck in park in front of our house, we were immediately all over each other. Our tongues were down each other's throats, rough like they were fighting. Our hands were grabbing at each other, trying desperately to remove the wet clothing from our bodies.

"I want you so bad. Let's go into the house," I managed to whisper through the heavy breathing.

"Good idea," he agreed.

Both of us were panting, trying to catch our breath like old dogs do when they realize they can no longer go for long walks anymore.

Once we were in the front door, we couldn't keep our hands off each other. We worked hard at getting the wet clothes off each other, and it was not easy!

"You look amazing, Lena," Bryan whispered.

We walked to the stairs with intentions of going up, but we never made it that far as Bryan laid me down on the stairs and began kissing me from my lips all the way down to my other lips!

"My, my, Ms. McAnderson, I guess you weren't lying when you said you wanted me bad." Then he whispered in my ear, "Do you want me to show you how bad I want you?"

"Yes. Please."

I was so wet from excitement that Bryan slid right in, but slowly. I positioned myself so that I had the ability to wrap my legs around his waist and he could go deeper as I grabbed his ass and assisted him in pushing harder against me. By the look on Bryan's face, I could tell it was working out well. With each movement, we both moaned in pleasure. As Bryan quickly slid in and out of me, I found myself yelling loudly, "Don't stop!" He pushed himself into me harder and harder until we both finally climaxed together. Bryan turned over onto his back, lying next to me on the stairs so that we were both staring up at the ceiling, trying to catch our breath and looking defeated.

"That was fucking amazing," I finally said, breaking the silence.

"Last one to their room is a rotten egg!" Bryan yelled, shoving me as he ran naked up the stairs.

"Um, no fair, cheater!" I managed to get out, laughing hysterically. "What if my dad had surveillance cameras installed throughout the house before he left, and he just watched us have sex on the staircase?"

"Really, Lena? Then your dad just got a free show of some really great sex!"

"You scummer!" I said, slapping his right arm before retreating to my room to get changed.

"Your dad would never consider installing any cameras to watch you, of all people," Bryan chuckled, following me into my room.

"What are you trying to…are you saying my dad thinks I am a prude?" I hit him again but this time in the left arm.

"Hey, you said it, not me…and ouch! That one really hurt," he said, rubbing his left arm. "So since that was *so amazing*, which are the words I believe you used to describe our sexual encounter, how about we snuggle together tonight and maybe—"

Before Bryan finished his sentence, I whacked him one more time in the sore left arm, not really thinking about it, and said, "Don't even go there! You got lucky once tonight. Don't push it!" I gave him fake anger eyes.

"Fine," he said, sounding defeated, and walked into his bedroom and closed the door.

———

The next morning when I was using the bathroom, I realized that I couldn't remember the last time I'd had my period. My heart sank, and I felt sick to my stomach at the thought. *What if I'm pregnant? That would be horrible! Bryan and I are not married. I'm definitely not ready for kids, and I'm sure Bryan isn't ready for kids. Heck, I don't even know if Bryan even wants to marry me or have kids.*

I began to really panic. *This is bad, really bad. What do I do?* I began taking deep breaths in and out. *What am I going to say to Bryan? Do I even tell him?* My mind was spinning.

"Maybe I'm just overreacting," I said to myself. A knock on the door startled me, and I let out a high-pitched scream.

"Are you okay in there? Who are you talking to?" Bryan asked with concern in his voice. "You've been in there for quite a while. Is there something I can get you?"

"Yeah, a new life!" I snapped.

"Okay, can I come in please?" Bryan pleaded.

"Sure," I said softly.

"Are you crying? Lena, what's wrong?"

Looking at Bryan with tears streaming down my face, I stammered out, "Please don't be mad at me, okay?"

"Um, okay," Bryan replied, sounding confused.

"I think I might be pregnant." I lifted my head quickly to see what Bryan's reaction was.

"Oh. Okay. Wow. Definitely not what I expected, but okay, are you sure?"

"Well, no," I said slowly. "I took a test and it showed positive, but I know there's a chance it could be a false positive, so I need to see a doctor to confirm it."

"Then let's call your doctor, set up an appointment, and we can go from there."

I was extremely surprised by Bryan's calm demeanor.

"See if you can set up an appointment this week and we can go on our lunch break. Sound good?"

"Really? You will go with me?"

"Of course I will, silly girl. Now come on and get ready before we are both late for work."

CHAPTER 47

Bethany

"So you're no good to me anymore. I'm sorry to do this, but I have to make sure you're dead before I throw your body out to the curb." He chuckled at the thought. *You idiot, there are no curbs out here. It is the country.*

"I don't have much time, so we need to make this quick and sweet," he said as he sliced her neck. However, very little liquid came out.

That's because she was already dead.

He cut the rope she was hanging from, and her body just crumpled on the ground like a rag doll.

"Okay, up you go over the shoulder. Don't go giving me a hard time, okay?" *Ha! I'm talking to a dead girl.*

Although it was daylight, he was going to take the chance and get rid of her body once and for all. He drove for about two hours to Winston before finally picking the spot where he would dump her at her final resting place.

Not a soul in sight.

He carried her lifeless body, wrapped in black garbage bags, deep into the wooded area. He threw her body into a heavily shaded spot and walked away, just leaving Bethany's body there as if it was actually a piece of garbage.

Now back to work I go.

Chance

When Chance walked through the door of Wesley's, he noticed everyone standing around looking somber.

"What's with all the long faces?" he asked.

"Hey, buddy, why don't you come into my office," Ray said, putting his hand on Chance's shoulder.

Both men walked into Ray's office as he gently closed the door.

"Ray, you're kind of freaking me out, dude. This is very unlike the perky Ray I know."

"Chance, we just got a phone call about a half hour before you walked in that Bethany's body was found in a park in Winston. They found her earlier today but couldn't locate any family members to give them the sad news, but they were able to find out that she was a stripper here at the club. Now I know you guys had some history, so I understand if you need to take some time off during this difficult time."

"Ray, stop. Stop. I don't need any time off. Am I upset? Yes, I cared about her, but did you forget that we also ended our nonexistent relationship?"

"So you don't need any time off?" Ray asked, sounding a bit relieved and confused at the same time.

"No, I'm good. Can I go get the bar ready before we open the doors?"

"Sure. If you're okay, then feel free. Some of the girls that knew her well did go home, so it may be a slow night."

"You will not hear any complaining from me," Chance laughed.

As the night went on, he realized he was a little sad that Bethany was gone. Not because he cared about her anymore, but the simple fact that someone just threw her body somewhere, like a piece of garbage, and left it there to rot.

One thing I know for sure is my hands are clean! So if the cops do come sniffing around, I have nothing to hide, Chance assured himself.

The night did turn out to be a slow one. As he was hanging out behind the bar with not much to do, he pulled up the internet on his phone and typed in, "Woman found dead at park in Winston."

A picture of Bethany popped up, and the story followed. With his hand over his mouth, he read about how she was strangled, her body mutilated, her throat cut.

"Can I get a drink over here? You okay? You look like you've seen a ghost!" joked a patron.

Four a.m. cannot come fast enough! Chance thought.

Thankfully, not many people were at the club, so there was a very good chance they could close their doors early. Chance didn't get his hopes up though. He just went back to looking things up on his phone and playing on the internet.

CHAPTER 48

Lena

"Would you stop shaking that leg already!" Bryan laughed.

"It's a nervous twitch. I can't stop. What if the doctor comes in and says the test is positive? How are we going to afford a baby?" I asked nervously, leg still shaking.

"Lena, shhhh—" Before Bryan could finish his sentence, there was a small knock on the door, which made my heart drop, not knowing what to expect. I held my breath as the doctor said, "I'm happy to let the both of you know that it's a false alarm. The test came out negative."

I jumped off the table into Bryan's arms, and we hugged for what seemed like forever.

"It's not unusual for a woman to go weeks, sometimes months without getting their period. We can have some tests done, and we'll keep an eye on it, but for now you're in the clear."

The walk back to the truck was quiet. I finally broke the silence by saying, "Well, that was quite the scare, huh?" Both of us just sat staring out the front window of the truck before Bryan started the engine. I couldn't tell if he was relieved or angry.

"Well, let's turn this not-so-fun, scary day into a fun day!" Bryan finally said. "Let's go look at puppies!"

"Puppies? Are you serious, or are you joking?" I asked with a confused look on my face.

"I am totally serious," Bryan said, still looking straight out the front window.

"Bryan, you know that's a big commitment. Are you sure that's what you want to do?"

Bryan gave me an almost-pissed-off look. "Um, did we not just walk out of a doctor's office thinking the whole time that we were having a baby?" He snapped, "I think I can handle a fucking puppy."

"Whoa! Okay. Sorry—" I started to say before Bryan cut me off.

"I'm sorry. I shouldn't have yelled at you. I guess I'm a little emotional, is all. Yes. I'm sure I want to get a puppy with you," Bryan said, holding my hand.

"Okay, then let's do this!" I said.

We shopped around for four hours before finding Chewie, a brown lab puppy that moved his mouth like he was constantly chewing on something. We both fell in love with him the moment we saw him. He was the only puppy who didn't follow all the others. He sat in the corner all by himself, that was until I whistled to get his attention and he strolled overlooking like he was chewing on the air, wagging his little tail.

When I picked him up, he snuggled right into my chest, then looked up and gave me sweet puppy kisses. I knew right then and there he was the one, the one that stole my heart. Bryan knew by the look on my face and my reactions that Chewie was the one, so six hundred dollars later we had our first puppy together.

We decided to celebrate Chewie's first night home by having a candlelight dinner, then watching the movie *Lady and The Tramp 2: Scamp's Adventure*, which we thought was a nice touch, although Chewie had his eyes closed most of the time.

I woke up the next morning to puppy kisses. Oh, that lovely puppy breath! The kisses then turned into nibbles on the fingers.

"Well, I guess I don't need an alarm to wake me up for work anymore," I said to Chewie.

I peeked into Bryan's room to see that he was still sleeping, so I decided to plop Chewie on top of his head. Little did I know, Chewie would begin to pee on the pillow next to Bryan's head.

"What the—" Bryan started to yell, throwing his arms in the air.

"Oh my gosh, I'm so sorry! I didn't know he needed to pee! I'll clean your sheets for you, I promise. It's a stinky morning shower," I said trying to make a joke, but the look on Bryan's face told me he wasn't having it.

After breakfast, Bryan and I decided we were going to walk to work today since it was nice outside. "You think Chewie will be okay in the crate for eight hours?" I asked.

I could tell Bryan could hear the concern in my voice as he grabbed my hand, squeezed it, and said, "Lena, I'll come home on my lunch break and let him out."

"What a huge relief! Thank you so much! I can't wait to tell everyone about our new baby. Furry baby, that is!" I said, excitedly bouncing up and down.

CHAPTER 49

Lena

I was stocking the shelves at work when I thought I caught sight of *him* walking by. *No,* I thought to myself. *If he had stuck around, I would've run into him by now, wouldn't I?*

When I turned the corner to stock the next aisle, I noticed Sandy, the new hire, also stocking the shelves. Although I didn't know her well, I couldn't hide my excitement about our new puppy, so I decided to tell her all about him.

"Hi, Sandy! How was your weekend?" I asked gently, hoping not to startle her.

Sandy stopped what she was doing and looked as if she was thinking about what to say. "It was okay," she finally responded, then continued on, "I really didn't do anything. I stayed home and watched TV. What about you? Lena, right?"

"Yes, it is Lena! My roommate, Bryan, and I adopted a puppy! A brown male lab." I couldn't contain my excitement, which was obvious from the huge smile on my face. I pulled up a picture on my cell phone to show Sandy, and she shrieked, "Oh my goodness, how cute! What did you name him?"

"Chance!" I shouted out loud.

"Well, that's a cute name for a—"

"No, no—" I interrupted, making Sandy jump.

"That's not his name, sorry. I didn't mean to startle you. His name is Chewie."

"Then who is Chance?" Sandy asked, puzzled.

I put my finger up, in a gesture for Sandy to hold her thought. "I'll be right back."

I could feel my heart pounding fast and hard in my chest. *Why am I getting this strange feeling again?* I wondered.

When I reached the end of the aisle, I slowly peeked around the corner, and there stood Chance. A hot flash ran right through my body. "He's still here! I can't believe it!" I muttered to myself.

"Excuse me," said a soft voice from behind, which made me jump and let out a yelp. "I'm so sorry, dear, I didn't mean to frighten you," apologized the little old lady. She needed me to show her where the chili mix was. I froze once I realized we needed to walk toward him.

Snapping back to reality, I looked at the little old lady and pleasantly replied, "Right this way." I led the way to the chili seasoning, which happened to be in the exact same place Chance was standing. The closer we got, the faster my heart raced.

Seriously, why in the world is this happening to me just at the sight of this guy, again, who by the way is still kind of a stranger to me? I tried reasoning with myself. I wasn't sure if I wanted him to see me or not. One second, I was wishing he would turn around and look at me, and then the next I was hoping we could slip right by without him seeing me.

When we arrived at the chili seasoning packets, I gestured toward them and then louder than normal said, "Here they are!" hoping to catch the attention of the man I not once, but twice, spilled a drink on. No response. *Really?* I thought, then realized he was browsing through a magazine. However, I couldn't resist anymore. I knew I didn't look my best, but I desperately wanted, needed, to say hi.

"Okay, okay, I can do this," I tried convincing myself. Just as I was about to say hi, I chickened out and quickly turned right, frowning with my head hanging down. I began walking away from him, then...

"Lena?"

I stopped dead in my tracks, my body frozen stiff like I'd just gotten caught stealing. My heart began to race again, but this time a smile began creeping across my face. In my head, I was screaming,

145

Yes! Yes! In actuality, I was like, "Hey! Chance, right?" playing dumb like I wasn't positive of his name.

"Yes, that's me! I wasn't really sure you would remember who I was," Chance said with what I like to believe was a bit of excitement in his voice.

"How can I possibly forget the first guy I ever spilled a drink on?" I giggled nervously, trying to be funny, but then immediately regretted saying it.

Seriously? I scolded myself, but then he surprised me by saying, "Don't forget you also almost tried to drown me in vodka." With that we both were laughing pretty hard, for me it was mostly because those were some embarrassing moments.

"So you work here," Chance said matter-of-factly rather than posing it as a question.

I couldn't help but stare at his lips as they moved when he was talking. *Oh my god, what's wrong with me? What the hell am I doing? Why does this guy, strange, have this type of effect on me? Hell, I didn't know him from Tom, Dick, or Harry. For all I know, he could be a serial killer.* But I still stayed and stared.

"Do you have a boyfriend?" he asked, catching me off guard.

"Yes. I mean no. No, not really," I managed to stammer.

"So is that a no?" he asked, looking confused.

"Correct, I don't have a boyfriend. Sorry about that." I could feel my face turn red.

"Great! Would you like to have a drink with me sometime?" Chance asked, rocking back and forth.

"Tonight?" I blurted out.

"Well, whenever you're available. And I said *have* a drink. Let's not get that confused with me wanting to *wear* your drink," he said, laughing. "I'm sorry, I just had to throw that in there, and the look on your face right now is priceless."

I wasn't sure what my face looked like at the moment, but hopefully it wasn't the deer-in-the-headlights look.

"I'm available tonight," I offered way too quickly—again.

"Sounds good! You know the bar Peeves, right?" he asked.

"Do I know Peeves?" I repeated the question. "Of course I know Peeves. I was born and raised in that bar," then when I noticed him laughing at my reply, I realized he was being sarcastic. *Duh, you spilled drinks on him twice in that bar.*

"Can we meet there at seven thirty tonight?" Chance asked with what sounded like hope in his voice, but I could've been reading him all wrong.

"Sure! It's a date!" I said a little too enthusiastically. *"It's a date?" Really, Lena? You're such a dork,* I thought to myself.

With that, Chance walked toward the front of the store to cash out, and I went back to stocking shelves, only this time with a huge smile on my face. That was until I began thinking about Bryan and Chewie and started to feel somewhat guilty. *But guilty for what? It's not like Bryan and I are dating! We just live together. Roommates. Roommates with benefits sometimes, but that doesn't mean I can't date, right? It's not really a real date anyway,* I argued with myself. *We are just going for a drink,* I reminded myself. This made me feel better. *It's just a meeting with a friend, for a drink.*

Why I felt like a little schoolgirl with butterflies in her stomach was beyond me. *Who was I kidding? I was so excited!*

CHAPTER 50

Lena

Bryan stood in his usual spot right outside the automatic doors of Frederick's, waiting for me to finish up.

"Hey, sunshine!" he said as I walked out. "What's the big smile for? That happy to see me?" he said jokingly.

"Of course!" I said, which was partially true. But it really was from my excitement about tonight with Chance. I did feel a bit guilty but decided not to bring anything up about Chance on our walk home together.

As Bryan and I finished up dinner, he asked, "So what movie will it be tonight?"

Before I could answer, Bryan picked Chewie up, pretended as if the puppy was talking, and said, "Let's watch *All Dogs Go to Heaven*," in a cute baby voice.

"Well, I, um, can't watch a movie tonight," I said nervously.

Bryan lowered Chewie from in front of his face, looking confused. "Why?" he asked, sounding a bit shocked.

"Well," I stalled, "remember that guy I spilled my drink all over when you and I went to Peeves? His name is Chance." I waited a couple of seconds for Bryan to respond.

"Yeah…" Bryan answered slowly with some sadness in his voice. This was the point I think he began to realize where the conversation was going.

"Chance asked me if I could meet him for a drink at Peeves tonight at seven thirty. Would you care if I go?" I asked, keeping my fingers crossed behind my back.

"No, no, not at all, Lena, why would I care? It's not like we are dating or anything," Bryan said sarcastically.

"That is what I told Chance! I knew you would totally understand!"

"Go, have fun! Have a drink for me," Bryan said.

Bryan

Although he was smiling when he told her to have fun, he truly wanted to beg Lena to stay home with him and Chewie. "Chewie and I will have some male bonding time." Bryan hoped the sadness he was feeling inside was not visible in his voice.

Bryan looked up when he heard Lena come downstairs after an hour of getting ready. He couldn't help but notice Lena was wearing his favorite red blouse of hers. He wanted so badly to ask Lena not to go, but instead he kissed her on the cheek and told her to have a good time.

Bryan sat with Chewie on his lap, on the couch, just staring at a black television screen. *I wonder what they are doing right now,* he thought. For hours, he sat watching the clock on the wall.

Why am I upset? he wondered to himself. *It's not like we're dating. I mean, I never did actually ask her out, so technically we're not a thing. We are just living together, just as friends.*

Bryan shook his head. He could feel his insides burning up with anger. "I'm the idiot that didn't ask her out, so it's my own damn fault!" he said out loud, throwing his arms in the air. "All right, Chewie, we're going to have a great guy night together, okay?" he asked as if Chewie was going to respond. Chewie's ears perked up at the sound of hearing his name and picking up the excitement in Bryan's voice. However, that excitement was short-lived as Bryan realized again that Lena was out with another man, which wasn't him.

His mind began wandering thinking about what they were doing, what they might be saying to each other. *I wonder if they're dancing together, like we did.* Then the thought of them kissing set Bryan off. Now he was just straight-up pissed.

CHAPTER 51

Lena

"So what's your story?" I finally got the nerve to ask Chance four drinks later. "You're a very good-looking man that showed up in a hole-in-the-wall bar in a remote town by yourself, and didn't even blink when a certain someone," pointing to myself, "managed to spill their drink all over the front of you. Not very many tall, dark, handsome strangers just stroll into Silver Tree Acres without some kind of story."

"How many tall, dark, and handsome men do you know?" Chance asked, smiling.

"Well, none," I said, confused at first. Then I realized he was messing with me, so I changed my answer to, "Not very many." I pressed on, curious. "So are you running from something, hiding from someone or something?"

"Whoa, whoa, whoa, cowgirl, slow it down. Why do I have to have a story? Couldn't I have just stumbled upon this quiet little town and decided to stay because I fell in love with the place?" Chance said defensively, but not in a mean way.

"That is highly unlikely," I said in a drunken slur, eyeing him up suspiciously. "However, if that's what you're going with, then I guess I'll believe you." With that, we both started laughing.

"So tell me, what's there to do in Silver Tree Acres? You seem like you know the place pretty well," Chance said winking.

"Well, you're right about that, as I was born and raised here, but good luck on trying to find something fun to do, unless you like horseback riding or four-wheeling through the fields," I joked.

"There isn't much excitement that happens in this quiet little town. But! Now that I think about it, the Silver Tree Acres yearly fair is coming up on Thursday. Would you care to join Bryan and me?"

"Bryan? He's the guy that you were with the first time I met you, right?"

"Yes, that's him. He and I actually just became roommates."

The look on Chance's face told me he was confused.

"It is a long story," I said looking down.

"Hey, I have all night. Let's hear the story," he said, looking interested.

"Okay, well, here it goes," I said, taking a deep breath and exhaling. "Bryan and I became very close friends, unfortunately at the time of my mother's death. At the actual wake to be exact. We realized then that we both had something in common, we both had lost a parent at a young age. From that day on we became besties. Bryan would walk with me every day to school. Eventually, he began driving, and we would drive together to school. Bryan's dad was an alcoholic and just decided one day that he was going to up and leave without telling anyone where he was going. He left Bryan all alone, basically to fend for himself.

"A few years after my mom had passed, I was able to work a job and could take care of myself, and my dad decided it was time for him to move on himself. He moved down to Florida to enjoy the rest of his retirement. So since Bryan and I were both were living alone, we thought it'd be a good idea that we move in together. It has been working for us so far."

"So the two of you never dated?" Chance asked, looking surprised.

"No, we never dated. He's basically like the older brother I never had. Okay," I said, after taking a big gulp of my beer. "Your turn! I told you mine, now you have to tell me yours."

"That almost sounds dirty," Chance said, laughing and almost choking on his beer. "I literally just happened to drive through here and fell in love with the town, so I decided to stay. That is the honest-to-God truth. I've been living in a small motel room for the past couple of months, and I pray every day that I won't be out on the street because my cash is running very low."

"Why don't you come stay with Bryan and I?" I suggested.

"With you and your boyfriend? I mean friend, roommate?" he stuttered, looking at me suspiciously, not sure if I was serious or not.

When I nodded yes, he stood up straight and said, "No thanks, that's very kind of you to offer, but I don't want to intrude."

"Who said you'd be intruding? I just invited you to stay," I said, taking another gulp of beer with a huge smile on my face.

"Okay, let me think about it," Chance said, smiling back.

After finishing up our last drink, we left Peeves and got in his car. When we pulled up to the front of my house, he grabbed both of my hands in his and said, "This really has been great. I hope we can do this again."

"Me too! Sooner rather than later would be nice." I felt a little embarrassed that I just vomited out my words, yet again.

Chance and I hugged before I exited the car. I turned and waved to him before walking through my front door.

"Hey, you're back!" Bryan said.

"Yes, I am," I said matter-of-factly, feeling a little tipsy from the alcohol.

"Did you have a good time?" Bryan asked.

"Yes, I did. We chatted for hours, like we were old friends just shooting the shit as if we had not seen each other in a while. It was really nice," I said, smiling. "Hey, you know how we were going to-do-card night this Wednesday? Would you care if I invited Chance over to join us?" I asked, clenching my teeth, holding my breath with one eye open, not sure what Bryan was going to say.

"No, I don't mind. He can come over."

"Awesome!" I squealed. "We are going to have so much fun. You are going to love him."

"I don't know about all that," Bryan said back. "What'd you guys chat about?"

I could sense Bryan was not really being his usual self, so I just played it safe by responding generically, "Anything and everything."

I felt it was best to call it a night. The moment just felt awkward. "I'm really tired, Bryan. I think I'm going to turn in for the night, if that's okay."

"Of course it's okay, why wouldn't it be? Have a good night," Bryan said, sounding bummed.

CHAPTER 52

Bryan

The next morning on our walk into work, Lena and Bryan were in midconversation, laughing with each other, when her phone rang. She covered the phone and whispered to him that it was Chance with a huge smile on her face.

When they arrived at Frederick's, he wasn't sure if Lena wanted him to stop and say goodbye or just keep on walking, but then she ended her conversation with Chance, apologized to him for being rude, then hugged him and thanked him for the walk.

As Bryan continued his walk to his workplace, Constantine's, he wondered if the walk back home was going to be the same. Thinking about this angered him. He shivered at the thought that this was going to be the new norm. Bryan shook his head to clear the thoughts as he knew he had a busy day ahead of him.

———

When five o'clock rolled around, Bryan headed over to Frederick's to pick Lena up. Just as he feared, Chance was there, sitting behind the wheel of a shitty-orange rusty sedan.

As soon as Chance spotted Bryan, he immediately struck up a conversation. "Hey, buddy, how's it going?"

"Good. It's going good," Bryan lied. "What are you doing here?" he asked.

"Oh, I thought I would surprise Lena and give her a ride home. Do you know if she gets out soon?"

Although Bryan really wanted to tell him to go fuck off, he answered nicely, "Yes, she should be out any second."

"Chance! Bryan!" Lena said, appearing excited to see the both of us here at the same time.

"Hey, beautiful girl!" Chance said to Lena. "I thought I'd surprise you. Maybe take you to go get some dinner?"

Bryan could tell by the way Lena responded that she was disappointed when she told Chance that he usually walked her home every day. At first Bryan's reaction was, *Yes! You tell him Lena! That's my girl!* But then he felt bad seeing how excited she was and decide to say, "Oh, no, no, no, you two go right ahead. Don't worry about me, I'll be fine. Go enjoy yourselves," Bryan said with a forced smile, waving them off.

Then surprisingly Chance asked, "Bryan, why don't you just come with us?"

Then Lena chimed in waving at me to get into the car with them.

My response once again was, "No, no, you two go ahead."

"Come on," Chance said, with a sad, pouty face.

Okay, that's just weird, Bryan thought, but then gave in, "Okay, fine," as he hopped in the back of the old rusty sedan.

———

The hours went by quickly as they ate, laughed, drank, and chatted it up at the Chickpea Bar and Grill.

"Okay, who wants to do one more shot before we go?" Bryan asked, slightly slurring his words.

"We do!" Chance and Lena sang in unison.

Then Chance raised his hand in the air like he wanted to ask a question "Wait! On second thought, I probably shouldn't. I have to get you guys back home and drive back to my hole-in-the-wall apartment," Chance said.

"Oh, stop it, you're welcome to stay with us tonight," Bryan said, putting his hand on Chance's shoulder.

"Well, okay then," Chance quickly agreed.

"One. Two. Three!" They clinked their shot glasses and then threw them back. The final shot of the evening. It felt like the three of them had been friends forever. The friendship seemed to come so naturally.

When they got back into the sedan, it hit them how intoxicated they actually were.

Before Chance started the car, he looked at Lena and Bryan with a serious look on his face and slurred, "Okay, all of us are going to have to work together to get home. Stay awake and stay alert."

When we pulled up to the front of the house, Chance looked at them and said, "I hope I didn't scare you guys with that drive home," joking.

Bryan, not sure if Chance was serious or not, responded, "Dude, we just went around the corner." It was eerily quiet for a moment until they all looked at one another and broke out in hysterics.

"We may be country, but we don't scare that easily," Lena said laughing.

As they opened the front door, Chewie greeted them, wagging his tail and giving kisses.

"Chance, meet Chewie! Chewie, this is Chance," Lena said.

"Are you sure you are okay with me staying here? I don't want to be a burden."

Before Chance could finish what he was saying, Lena had cut him off. "Don't be silly, we wouldn't have offered if we didn't want you here."

I'm not quite sure I feel the same way, Bryan thought to himself.

"You guys are really awesome. I'm so lucky to have met the two of you. In the morning, I must start shopping around for a new apartment. If you guys know of any, please let me know," Chance said sleepily, lying on the couch.

"Hopefully I don't regret this, but why don't you come live with us?" Bryan suggested.

"Seriously?" he sat straight up, staring at Lena and me. "I really didn't think Lena was serious when she offered the other night."

Bryan, although smiling, was shocked and a bit mad for not knowing this tad bit of information that apparently transpired over their date the other night. "Oh really? Look at that, Lena and I are on the same page," he replied sarcastically, looking directly at Lena.

"In the morning, I will give you my key. You can go make a copy of it and start to move your things in while we are at work," Lena suggested, eyeing Bryan up for his approval.

"Absolutely," Bryan chimed in, then said good night and walked upstairs toward his room.

————

The next day, after Bryan and Lena got out of work, and they walked through the front door a fabulous-aroma-filled the house. Chance literally had only two suitcases that he was living out of, which were still sitting by the front door. Bryan and Lena walked into the kitchen and could not help but laugh as Chance had on a white apron that had the words "Kiss the Chef" on the front of it, and he was doing a little dance. He made himself right at home.

"Welcome home, hard workers!" Chance greeted them.

"What smells so good in here, Chance?" Lena asked, looking around.

"That would probably be my famous meatloaf," Chance said, pointing over to the stove. "I timed everything perfectly," he said excitedly. "We can eat right now. What to drink?"

"Wine," Bryan and Lena replied in unison. "It helps us relax after a long day," Bryan said, and Lena just smiled back at him in agreement.

CHAPTER 53

Lena

After we finished the wonderful dinner our new roommate made for us, we went to the junk room off the living room and started clearing it out for Chance.

"I know it's not real big, but it should do the job," I said.

"This is perfect! I'm only going to sleep in here." Chance laughed. "I'll just have to buy a bed and dresser now."

We spent the next few hours working our dinner off.

As we were winding down and getting ready to go to bed, I caught a glimpse of Chance taking off his shirt. *Wow,* was all I thought. *He is in really great shape.* Then for a hot second I thought that having him live here might be a bad idea. While I was walking away, Chance startled me when he said "Good night" before he plopped down onto the couch in the living room.

"See you in the morning," I said, blushing.

———

Suddenly I jumped awake in the middle of the night. In my best lingerie, I quietly tiptoed downstairs, hoping that Chance would really like it and not turn me away. I was so wet and could not stop thinking about him. When I walked into the living room, there he was all sprawled out on my couch wearing nothing but gray boxer briefs. His body was so beautiful.

I took it upon myself to slide over the bottom of the couch, and I slowly crawled up his body, kissing each part of him, starting from the knees up. His body began responding as I hoped it would. When I got to his boxer briefs, I grabbed them with my teeth and slowly pulled them down, releasing what I wanted. As I wrapped my tongue around his hard penis and moved up and down, he surprised me by jumping up, flipping me over, and violently caressing my soft spot with his tongue, making me more wet than I already was. He could not resist anymore and was inside of me, exactly where I wanted him to be.

"You feel so good," he whispered into my ear. Shortly after we started, I began to orgasm, shaking uncontrollably, breathing heavily. "Just like at the cabin." My eyes flew open.

"What? What? What's wrong?" Bryan asked, looking at me confused. "You were so into it, what happened? Did I do something wrong?"

"Oh my god, Bryan, I thought…I thought…" I couldn't get the words out of my mouth as I was still shocked that it was Bryan in bed with me and not Chance.

"Lena, what's the matter?" Bryan asked, sounding worried.

"Never mind. Can you just please go now?" I said, sounding a bit more irritated and harsher than I intended to be.

"I'm so sorry," Bryan said, getting dressed. "I came to snuggle with you, and you got all touchy-feely, so I took that as you wanted to do more."

"Okay, well, how about next time, I don't know, make sure I'm actually awake before having sex with me."

"Are you mad at me?" Bryan asked, sounding like a little kid.

"No, I'm not," I replied, feeling kind of guilty, because I did enjoy it. It just turned out not to be the person I anticipated it to be. "But really, please, don't sneak in here anymore to snuggle unless we discuss it prior to happening," I said much more calmly.

"Okay, Lena. I would never intentionally hurt you. Ever!"

"I know, Bryan. Now go to sleep, sneaky-ass." I plopped my head back down on my pillow, feeling a little exasperated.

———

The next morning, I was woken up by Chewie giving me a bath with his tongue. I lay there for a couple of minutes and just stared at the wall, thinking about what had happened the previous night.

I can't believe I had that dream about Chance, on the very first night he stays with us, and during that exact same time I was having sex with Bryan thinking it was Chance. Am I losing my shit or what?

I was kind of pissed at Bryan, but I really couldn't be because I must have done something to lead him on somehow for him to think it was okay to do what he did. It was awfully strange, though, that he decided he wanted to snuggle suddenly last night.

Well, it was over and done with. I needed to just let it go. Today was a new day. Living with two men now was going to be interesting.

When I made my way down to the kitchen, both Bryan and Chance were up, and breakfast was served. "Wow! Good morning!" I said, looking from Bryan to Chance, thinking, *This is a little weird.*

"So, Chance, how did you sleep last night?" I asked, looking at Bryan and giving him a look like, "Don't you dare say anything about what transpired last night between the two of us."

"I slept like a baby for the first time in months," he replied, sounding very happy.

"Great. Remember, tonight is game night," I reminded the boys.

"So who comes to game night?" Chance asked while lifting Chewie onto his lap.

"We each invite just a couple of coworkers over, so we usually have about six to eight people, depending on if they show up," Bryan responded.

"We play games like Scat, Taboo, Threes, and Cards Against Humanity," I chimed in with Bryan.

"I'll take care of cleaning up so that you guys can head out to work," Chance insisted. "I'm going to spend my day looking at bedroom sets today."

As Bryan and I were rushing out the door, a thought came to mind. "Chance?"

"Yes?" he yelled over running water.

"Do you have a job?" I asked, realizing this probably should've been one of our very first conversations before he moved in, but I guess when you've had a lot to drink, you don't really think rationally.

"Yes," he replied.

Before I could ask where, Bryan dragged me out the front door.

CHAPTER 54

Chance

"Hey, stranger! How's it going?"

"Wow, am I glad to hear a familiar voice!" Chance said with a smile on his face. "Remember that girl, Lena, that almost drowned me with vodka at that bar Peeves?"

"Kind of," Leeza replied but didn't sound too sure.

"Well, Lena and her roommate, Bryan, offered me a room at their house to stay in, at least until I can get back on my feet. Actually, today I am going to look for a bedroom set."

"That's great! What do they think about you working at a strip club?" Leeza asked.

"Actually, they don't know that I work at a strip club. Yet. It's funny that you bring that up because neither of them asked me if I had a job until this morning when they were running out the door on their way to work. Crazy, right?"

"I can't believe they trust you enough that they left you there in their home," Leeza said, teasing.

"Ha-ha, very funny. I miss being home, but it sure is peaceful here. I think I can definitely get used to this little town. It is amazing the difference between here and Cloverfield. I went from the fast-paced city life to a quiet country town. It's a big change. Speaking of which, how's it going over there in Maine?" Chance asked with some distress in his voice.

"Well, as a matter of fact, since you asked, your beautiful mug has made it on the front of the newspaper and a couple of magazines here with the caption 'Have you seen this man?'" Leeza said nervously, waiting to hear his response.

"You're joking, right? You're messing with me?" Chance asked with a nervous laugh. "Your delayed response is very reassuring," Chance said as he could hear Leeza take a deep breath before answering.

"Amanda's parents are convinced that you intentionally poisoned their daughter. They think you left Maine to hide."

"Seriously? Yes, I left, but not because I was guilty. You suggested that this was a good idea. You said the finger was going to be pointed at me. I didn't do anything wrong," Chance said, sounding defeated. "You didn't tell anyone where I am, did you?"

"Okay, now it is my turn to say 'Seriously?' Come on now. You know me. Your secret location is safe with me, and you're right, I did think leaving was the best thing for you to do. You'll be fine, you're in the middle of nowhere," Leeza said jokingly.

"I can't believe her parents could think I would ever do something like that to Amanda. I loved her, and I was always nice to them. I think they never really liked me, but they probably just pretended to because I asked their daughter to marry me," Chance said, looking down at the floor with sadness in his voice. "I never intended to hurt her."

"Chance, I know that. I'm so sorry for spoiling your mood," Leeza apologized.

"Don't apologize, it's totally not your fault. I'm the one who asked how everything was going there, and you were just being honest answering my question."

"Well, good luck with your shopping today. I will not tell a soul that I talked to you. Stay cute! I love you. Bye!"

Chance couldn't quit fathom what he had just learned, but it wasn't going to keep him from moving forward with his life. He had done nothing wrong.

Or had he?

CHAPTER 55

Lena

As Chance, Bryan, and I sat at the dining room table waiting for our guests to arrive, I remembered I hadn't had the opportunity to ask Chance where he worked, so I thought now was a good time to have that conversation. I was curious and excited to find out until he replied, "Wesley's."

"The gentlemen's club?" I blurted out. "Of all places to work, you chose to work in a strip club?" I said with a bit of irritation in my voice.

Chance, not sensing my sarcasm, looked at us as though this was good news, that we would be excited that he had a job. That was, until he saw my face and his smile disappeared quickly.

"There weren't that many places to choose from in this town. Plus, I have some bartending experience."

"I think it's awesome," Bryan said, high-fiving Chance.

Before I could even get another word in, the doorbell rang. I opened the front door and began greeting everyone. As I was about to shut the front door, this tall, beautiful, model-type blonde was walking up our porch stairs, and I was just about to ask her if she was lost when Bryan rushed past me, almost knocking me over to get to her. I couldn't help but stare at her as she walked into our house. She had perfectly curled blond hair, gorgeous lips that were covered in red lip gloss, and boobs that must have been at least a double D and were practically jumping out of her cute little red top.

I was very confused as to who this chick was. I had never even heard anything about her before. If anything, I would've thought

164

maybe Chance invited her from the strip club. I definitely was not expecting Bryan to go greet her.

As I closed the front door and turned to go to the table, I saw Bryan grab her hand and walk over to me. "Lena, this is Jocelyn. She works with me at Constantine's."

"Nice to meet you," Jocelyn said, holding her hand out.

"Hi" was all that came out of my mouth as I stared at her boobs. They were just...so...there!

Two bombshells in a row. First, I find out Chance works at the one and only strip club in town, and then Bryan brings home this gorgeous girl, which I still can't put together how she works at Constantine's, a construction-type environment. I couldn't help but wonder why he never mentioned her before.

I smiled to hide the confusion I was feeling inside. "Thank you everyone for coming! Most of you know each other, but we have two new guests I would like to welcome to our game night. That is Chance, who is our newest roommate, and Jocelyn, who apparently works with Bryan." After that introduction, I quickly sat in my chair at the table.

I began to explain to everyone at the table how Bryan and I met Chance and what our current living situation was, but I was caught off guard when I noticed the blond chick, Jocelyn, whispering to Chance and then giggling. This didn't sit well with me, and I took myself by surprise when I blurted out, "I'm sorry, is something funny that the two of you would like to share with the rest of us?" *Wow, that sounded really bitchy*, I thought.

"Not really, Jocelyn was just saying how she couldn't believe I was single. I'm sorry, I didn't mean to be a distraction," replied Chance. "Please continue."

I wasn't sure why this bothered me. Was I jealous? Why?

As I was handing out the cards for our first game, I couldn't help but notice Jocelyn's hand move under the table in Chance's direction at the same time that Bryan was flirting with her. I became so distracted that I lost count of the cards I was dealing. "I'm so sorry, everyone. I screwed up," I said, embarrassed, picking up the dealt cards.

"Are you okay, Lena?" Chance asked.

"Yes, I'm fine, I just lost count, no big deal. I promise it won't happen again." I giggled, trying to act like everything was okay, but really my mind was reeling about this new revelation of Jocelyn. I just didn't understand why Bryan never told me about her.

In the middle of playing Cards Against Humanity, blondie decided to yell, "Let's do shots!" so of course she became the center of attention again. Bryan didn't hesitate as he ran over to our stock of liquor and started pouring and handing out shots to everyone.

I wasn't mad about it.

Or maybe I was. But it's not like doing shots is something new. I think I was just upset because it was her idea. *You know, you're being ridiculous,* I said to myself. *Stop this craziness and just join in and have fun.*

A couple of shots later, I seemed to have calmed down some. That was until it appeared that Jocelyn was leaning in to kiss Chance, but then she jumped up and announced that she had to pee. Out the corner of my eye, I saw Jocelyn wave to get Bryan's attention. I watched Bryan get up and follow her up the stairs, and then they disappeared into the bathroom together.

I debated with myself whether or not to get up and "accidentally" walk in on them, but instead I decided to jump into Jocelyn's seat next to Chance and turned on the charm. One minute we were having a conversation about his stupid job, and then next thing I knew our tongues were intertwined.

"Are you fucking kidding me?" Bryan yelled as he walked down the stairs, scaring me so badly I literally jumped right out of my seat.

"Can I talk to you?" Bryan asked angrily, grabbing me by my arm, leading me toward the kitchen.

"What's your problem?" I snapped.

"Me? You want to know what my problem is? What is your problem? I can't believe you were just kissing our new roommate right in front of everyone! In front of me for, crying out loud," Bryan cried.

Of course I was worked up from him yelling at me, so I screamed back at him, "Are you joking? You were just in the bathroom with that blond bimbo, that by the way you failed to ever mention works with you!"

"Lena, she called me into the bathroom to ask me about Chance! Not to make out with me! I told her he was available, but apparently I was wrong."

I wanted to stop Bryan from walking away from me, but I honestly didn't know what to say. He made his way upstairs as I was walking back out to the table in the dining area. I was embarrassed, sad, and happy all at the same time. Embarrassed because I couldn't believe that this all took place in front of our group of friends. Sad because I think I really hurt Bryan, and happy that Chance kissed me and not Jocelyn.

Boy, was I confused!

Bryan stood at the top of the stairs and looked spaced out, just staring into thin air.

Chance looked upset too. He got up out of his seat, walked right past me without looking, and out the front door he went.

Game night ended abruptly.

I escorted everyone out before retreating to my own room.

Chapter 56

Gina

Anger. Red. Hurt. He had never felt like this before. Not this bad. Not even when his dad had treated him like crap. He felt the need to hurt someone. Physically. This feeling kind of scared him. Lena was going to be his and his only. How dare that dickhead get upset. Who does that bastard think he is!

He kicked the stones on the dirt road, making his way toward the Silver Tree Acres annual fair. As he walked into the entrance for the fair, he had only one goal in mind. To meet a pretty girl. It would help him get over the embarrassment of tonight. The night was thankfully still early enough that he had a good two hours to find someone. He headed straight toward the beer tent. It was packed.

The beers were going down much too smoothly. He had this overwhelming anxiousness that he was unsure what to do with. Chugging one beer after the other, he was feeling very depressed until this beautiful brunette walked right up to him. He did a double take to make sure it was him that she was there for.

"Hi, my name is Gina," she said, extending her hand.

"Nice to meet you, my name is Greg. Do you live here in Silver Tree Acres?" he asked.

"No, actually I'm just here visiting my cousins."

"Perfect," he said, not realizing he said it out loud.

"What's perfect?" Gina asked.

"Oh, nothing. I was just thinking out loud. My apologies."

"No apologies needed here," she said, yanking him out onto the makeshift dance floor, which was just a patch of on grass under the tent in front of the band playing.

As the words of "Sweet Home Alabama" rang through the air, he envisioned his hands around Gina's neck, and not in a lovey-dovey kind of way. He wanted to put his hands around her neck as tightly as he could and squeeze until she took her last breath.

If only Gina knew what he was thinking, but she didn't, and she took him up on leaving the beer tent to continue the party. He told her his friends were having a party in a barn down the road. She in her drunken state had no idea what she just got herself into.

"So where's this place again?" Gina asked.

"Right up this path. We're almost there."

When they reached the barn, Gina noticed there were no lights on inside, only the one light barely hanging on the outside above the barn doors. Sensing that she was starting to resist, he grabbed her by her wrist and yanked her inside the barn with him. She wanted to scream, but she was so scared that she literally froze in place. Her mouth was open, but nothing was coming out.

He wrestled her to the ground, violently ripping off her clothes and raping her. Just like he envisioned, he put his hands around her neck. He enjoyed watching her struggle to get air while he choked her.

Not until her body went limp did he climax.

He stood up to adjust his clothes and looked down at her lifeless body, scolding her, "That's what you get for embarrassing me in front of everyone."

CHAPTER 57

Lena

The yelling woke me right out of my sleep. I jumped out of bed and ran out into the hallway when I realized it was Bryan, so I went right into his room.

"Bryan!" I yelled. "Bryan! Wake up! You're having a nightmare. Wake up!" I was shaking him for what felt like minutes before he finally opened his eyes.

"What's up?" Bryan asked in a groggy voice. As he lifted his blankets to sit up, I couldn't help but notice the dirt all over his clothes.

This was the first time I had seen Bryan since last night, when he went to his room after our argument.

"I'm sorry for what I did last night. I hope you'll forgive me," I said sincerely.

As Bryan and I were talking, we heard the downstairs door open and then close and Chewie barking. I looked at Bryan. "Must be Chance? Did he go somewhere last night?"

We continued to listen but didn't hear anything else.

"So back to what I was saying, I had a lot to drink last night, and I wasn't thinking...Bryan? Bryan? Are you okay? You have that creepy blank stare on your face again like you did last night."

Bryan turned and looked at me. "What in the world are you talking about?" he asked, placing his hand on his forehead. "My head's killing me. What time is it?"

"Hey, champ, what's going on?" Chance asked, walking into Bryan's room, then up to Bryan and doing some weird man handshake. "You're a mess, bro, why're you all dirty? Did you go out last night?"

"Actually, I did. I left to take a walk to try and calm down some, but I must've really drunk a lot because I remember walking out our front door, but then after that's a big fat blur. I don't even know what time I got back here. What about you, did you just walk in?" Bryan asked Chance.

"I did. I felt so bad about everything that went down last night that I also left to clear my head."

"Chance, what time's it?"

"It's 6:00 a.m."

"Oh, man, I'm going back to bed. You should too!" Bryan said to Chance, yawning.

"Okay. Try not yelling in your sleep again and startling me awake," I giggled then walked back over to my room. I was just too tired to ask any questions about what either of them did when they left the house.

Bryan finally strolled down the stairs around 8:30 a.m.

"Chance and I already showered, so the bathrooms all yours," I let Bryan know. "Also, Chance has offered me a ride into work so that I won't be late. I hope that's okay." I worried a little about what his reaction to that would be, but all Bryan did was nod his head.

"We can all have dinner together later, okay?" I suggested rather than asked.

"Yeah, okay," Bryan replied quietly, holding his head.

"I hope you feel better," I said before following Chance out the front door.

"You think Bryan is okay?" Chance asked.

"Yes, he'll be fine, he's just a little hungover from last night."

"I meant, do you think he's upset with us, about what took place last night?"

"He's a big boy. He'll get over it. We didn't do anything wrong," I said defensively.

"I'm sorry, I didn't mean to upset you," Chance said.

"No, I'm sorry, I didn't mean for that to come out the way it did. Thank you so much for giving me a ride this morning. And don't worry, everything will be fine."

"Okay! See you at dinnertime!" Chance waved from the rusty orange sedan as I walked through the front doors of Frederick's.

———

I got a surprise at the end of my shift when I walked out to Bryan's truck. Chance was sitting in the passenger seat. This put a big smile on my face. I was really worried how things were going to be going forward, but I didn't want to tell Chance that earlier.

I hopped into the truck and squeezed my butt in between the two of them. I felt like we were three peas in a pod. I was looking forward to going home and eating dinner. When we walked through the front door, the smell of garlic tickled my nose. Turns out the boys had hung out all day, made up, and decided to surprise me by cooking dinner. Although it was only spaghetti and garlic bread, it was okay with me. I was starving. Knowing that the boys were getting along was such a huge relief to me.

The only part of the night that sucked was when Chance said he had to go back to work tonight. I had briefly forgotten about where he worked. But who was I to tell him where he could and couldn't work? I just had to suck it up and deal with it.

CHAPTER 58

Chance

"Welcome back!" Ray yelled when Chance walked through the doors.

"Hey, Ray, you miss me?" Chance laughed.

"It has only been three days. You act like it has been a month," Ray shot back.

When Chance went into the changing room in the back to say hi to the girls, he noticed they all had somber faces, like something bad had just happened.

"Hello, ladies! Have you missed me?" he joked, hoping to lighten the mood.

The girls came running over to give Chance a welcome-back hug. All but one. Kathleen, a.k.a. Pixie. However, it didn't look like she wanted to talk, so he decided not to bother her. If she decided she wanted to talk about it, she certainly would.

While Chance was tending bar, he looked up and noticed while on stage, Kathleen looked worried and kept glancing around the crowd, like she was looking for something or someone.

Strange, he thought. *Hope everything's okay. She is such a nice girl.*

Then some drunk dude decided to be a jackass and yell across the room, "Would someone please give this chick a happy pill or something?" He made his way over to the bar. "What the hell is wrong with that girl? They need to get her off the stage."

"Sir," Chance said calmly, "please don't be a jerk. Can't you tell the girl is having a bad day?"

"I don't give two shits if she is having a bad day. I paid good money to see some happy strippers, not some fuckin' Debbie Downer." Before Chance could say anything else, the man walked away.

When Kathleen finished her time on stage, Chance decided to go ask her if she was okay. When he entered the changing room, for the second time that day, Kathleen was looking at her cell phone and bawling her eyes out.

"Hi, Kathleen. I don't want to pry, but I'm worried about you. You don't have to answer this if you don't want to, but is everything okay? Is there anything I can do for you?"

Kathleen got up and hugged Chance, whispering, "Thank you. My cousin flew here from North Carolina to spend some time with me. She went to the fair yesterday without me because I had to work here last night. When I got home this morning, she wasn't there. As much as I don't want to think negative thoughts, I haven't heard a word from her since she went. Even if she decided to stay somewhere else, she would've at least called me. I called her phone and left so many messages that her inbox is full."

Kathleen took a deep breath.

"I called my aunt to see if maybe she flew back home, but my aunt said she didn't go home, and she also has not heard from her. I think she's missing."

"What's her name?"

"Gina, Gina Hedlidge."

"What does she look like?" Chance asked, concerned.

"She's not really tall, maybe five-four, she's a brunette, and her eyes are hazel but look mostly green," Kathleen said through sniffles.

"Maybe she'll show up. Maybe she just drank a little too much last night and passed out somewhere trying to sleep off her hangover. We've all been there," Chance said, smiling, hoping to make a little light of the situation. Unfortunately, it just made her cry a little harder.

He hugged her and told her to go home and that he'd let Ray know.

"If you don't hear from her by tomorrow, let me know. I'll do whatever I can to help. Make signs, hang them, walk around town, talk to neighbors," Chance offered. "Now go home, get some sleep. Sounds like we may have a busy day tomorrow."

"Are you saying you think she is dead?" Kathleen asked, shocked.

"No, no, no, that's not what I meant. Just go home. Get some sleep. I'll be in touch."

"Thank you, Chance, for caring. You're a good man. Bethany didn't deserve you," Kathleen said before turning and walking out the back door.

The last comment made Chance smile. Bethany hadn't deserved him.

CHAPTER 59

Lena

Bryan had called in sick to work again this morning, which was very unlike him. He said he felt like he'd been hit by a truck. He only got out of bed to take some medicine and then went right back to bed.

Hours later, as he made his way downstairs, I greeted him with a "Good morning, sunshine! Glad you can join us for dinner!"

"Dinner? I thought it was breakfast time." Bryan sounded astonished. "Apparently I slept for some time."

"I can't believe you actually slept that long. I wonder if you're coming down with something," I said.

"You must have partied really hard the other night when you went out," Chance teased.

"Maybe someone slipped a roofie in my drink," Bryan joked.

"Come give us a hand with dinner," Chance offered.

Bryan set up the table in the dining room as we decided to eat there instead of the kitchen table for once. After bringing dinner to the table, we turned on the six-o'clock news and were immediately shocked to find out there was another murder in Silver Tree Acres.

"You know, I moved to this quiet little town because I thought it was safe, but it appears there may be a serial killer lurking here. How many people have been killed already?" Chance asked without much concern in his voice before shoving spaghetti into his mouth.

"I know, usually here in Silver Tree you die of old age, alcoholism, or a fatal illness such as cancer, like my mom. But murder? It's kind of freaking me out."

"Lena, you're in good hands," Bryan assured me, looking over to Chance, who nodded his head in agreement with his mouth still full of spaghetti.

"Can you turn up the volume?" Chance asked Bryan, who had the remote control right next to him. Then clear as day, the newscaster said, "An unidentified woman whose body was discovered in the fields behind the fairground this afternoon by three teenagers walking, cutting through a path on their way home from school. The victim's name will not be released until authorities have contacted the family."

All three of us just looked at one another and didn't have to say one word as to how we were feeling. It was written all over our faces.

"Murder at the fairgrounds is way too close to home for me," I said nervously.

"Don't worry, Lena, you'll be fine," both guys reassured me once again.

The news anchor continued with the grueling unpleasant details of the murder, stating that the victim had been completely naked, beaten, skull smashed in, had been sexually assaulted, and had what appeared to be finger marks on her neck, indicating she might have died from asphyxiation.

Bryan suddenly jumped out of his seat, startling Chance and me, as he ran up to the bathroom and regurgitated his dinner.

I looked at Chance then just tapped his hand as a gesture to say I was going to go check on Bryan.

I walked upstairs to the bathroom and knocked gently on the door, asking Bryan if he needed anything. I peeked my head inside. "This flu bug you have seems pretty nasty. I'll grab you some water, and I suggest you go lie back down."

Chewie usually could sense when someone didn't feel good, but for some odd reason this time he seemed to keep his distance from Bryan.

After dinner, Chance and I cleaned up the dishes, and as we were finishing up, Bryan came into the kitchen and asked me if I would take a walk with him. I gladly accepted the invite.

I originally started to walk toward the barn, but Bryan grabbed my waist and uttered, "Let's go this way instead." It seemed a bit odd, but I really didn't think twice about it at the time.

"Lena, I want to apologize for the way I acted the other night at game night. I should've never made that big of a deal over you and Chance. It was foolish of me, and I hope you'll accept my apology." Bryan grabbed my left shoulder, swung me around to face him, and extended his arms out to me, gesturing for a hug.

"Of course I forgive you, Bryan. Honestly, I thought it was kind of cute that you were a little jealous," I said, messing with him.

"Really?" he asked, his eyes getting big.

"Okay, let's not let that go to your head," I said, laughing.

When we made our way back toward the house and the barn was in sight, an idea popped into my head. "Do you think we should renovate the barn? Maybe turn it into something useful?" I proposed.

"Like what? What's that little brain of yours pondering right now? I think it's perfectly fine the way it is," Bryan responded.

When we walked through the front door, Chewie greeted us with his tail wagging and lots of kisses.

Chance was sitting at the dining room table and had this look of concern on his face like something was really bothering him.

Bryan said he was going to lie back down as he still didn't feel quite right, so I joined Chance back at the table.

"Is everything okay?" I asked.

"I was just thinking about something that happened at work last night. One of the dancers had said her cousin came into town and that she went to the county fair and never came home afterwards. I hope to God the woman they found wasn't her cousin."

"Oh my god, that would be awful. I hope that it's not her either."

Chance and I relocated from the dining room table to the couch to watch a little more television before he had to get ready for work. As we were watching *Family Feud*, it was interrupted by breaking news: "The young woman found murdered this afternoon has been identified as Gina Hedlidge from North Carolina." A picture popped up on the screen of her.

The remote dropped out of Chance's hand, and he turned white as a ghost.

"Chance, are you okay?" I asked nervously. The quick change in his mood kind of frightened me.

"Chance, is that the dancer's cousin?"

Without answering the question, he ran upstairs and slammed the bathroom door shut.

What the heck is happening with these boys? I thought to myself.

Without another thought about it, I continued watching TV by myself the rest of the night.

CHAPTER 60

Lena

"Rise and shine, everyone!" Bryan yelled from the stairway.

I slowly lifted my head to see that it was only 6:50 a.m., meaning I still had ten more minutes before I needed to get up. On a good note though, Bryan sounded like he was feeling better and was in a great mood.

My eyes started to look at the back of my eyelids, that was until Bryan ran into my room and plopped on me, making me scream for dear life, which in return clearly scared Chewie and Chance, as Chewie flew in the room and jumped on the bed to join us and I heard Chance run out of his room. As he made his way up the stairs, he was yelling "I'm coming! I'm coming! Are you—" Before he finished his sentence, his question was answered when he walked into my bedroom.

"Seriously!" Chance said shaking his head, sounding a little annoyed as Bryan and I lay on my bed laughing our asses off and Chewie wagging his tail.

"We're sorry, Chance," I apologized through giggles.

"Okay, you two, I may have got mine, but you just wait! You'll get yours when you are least expecting it. Two, or should I say three, can play at this game!" Chance said, half-asleep, rubbing his eyes as he stood there in his Calvin Kleins.

———

When I walked out of Frederick's at 5:10 p.m., there was Bryan, on time as usual and standing there chatting up Margie, who was out on her cigarette break. When he looked up and noticed me walking toward them, a big bright smile appeared on his face. That smile melts my heart, puts me at ease, and makes me feel safe.

Sometimes I truly feel Bryan is my soul mate. However, there is a small part of me says that Chance came into my life for a reason. The thought tugged at my heart, but I tried not to let it show as Bryan and I walked home together.

While we made our way toward Webster Lane, we noticed Chance's rusty sedan drive off in a hurry.

Bryan turned toward me, looking confused. "I thought we were supposed to have dinner tonight? The three of us."

"I tried calling him earlier, but he didn't answer his phone. Maybe he just has some errands to run beforehand."

When we arrived at the house, there was a handwritten note on the dining room table, which looked like it was written in a hurry, but not any reason to set off any alarms. The note simply said, "Something came up. Sorry had to run. Fed Chewie."

Bryan and I attached little importance to it and continued with preparing dinner. We agreed we would just make a plate for Chance so that he could eat later when he got back from his running around.

Only he did not come home.

We became worried.

We called his phone several times and left him a bunch of messages, but in a lost effort we never got ahold of him.

"Maybe he ran out of time running errands and had to go straight to work," I suggested.

It wasn't until the next morning that we saw Chance.

CHAPTER 61

Lena

Chance walked in the front door as we were getting ready to walk out it.

"Chance!" Bryan and I both said at the same time, getting ready to ask him where he had been, but he just held up his hand and said he didn't want to talk about it right now.

Respecting his wishes, we continued on our way quietly.

"What do you think happened?" Bryan asked, looking over at me.

I just shook my head. "I have no clue."

———

Bryan

A police car pulled up and parked right in front of the entrance of Constantine's. Two uniformed Silver Tree Acres police officers walked up to two employees just exiting the building. "Good morning, folks, we're looking for a Bryan Mills. We received some information that this is his place of employment. Do either of you know who he is?"

Just as they shook their heads in unison that they were not familiar with someone by that name, Bryan and Jocelyn walked out the front doors of Constantine's.

"What's wrong, Officers?" Jocelyn asked.

"We are looking for a Bryan Mills," they began to say.

"I'm Bryan Mills," Bryan said without hesitation. "How can I help you?"

Ignoring Jocelyn, the officers told Bryan he needed to come down to the police station with them as they had some questions they needed to ask him. Bryan, unconcerned, calmly responded, "Okay, no problem."

"Bryan, call me later!" Jocelyn shouted as the police officers escorted him to the police car.

"May I ask what this is about, Officers?" Bryan asked.

"Let's leave all of the questions for at the station," the redheaded officer replied while helping Bryan into the backseat of the police car.

When they arrived at the police station, they helped Bryan get out of the back seat of the police car, and they headed straight in and pointed to a door that was labeled Interrogation Room.

"Before we begin, would you like anything to drink?" Officer Brent asked.

"No, thank you," Bryan calmly declined.

"Okay, so let's get started. Where were you last Wednesday evening?"

"Let's see. We—"

"Who is we?" the redheaded officer, Officer Kerry, cut Bryan off.

"My roommates, Chance, Lena, and I. We had a few friends over, and we played a couple of games. Afterward, when everyone had left, Jocelyn, the girl who just walked out of Constantine's with me today, texted me afterwards asking if I could meet up with her at the Silver Tree Acres fair. I texted her back saying I would."

The dark-haired officer, Officer Brent, stopped Bryan before he continued, "So you're telling us you were at the fair Wednesday evening to meet up with Jocelyn?"

"That's correct," Bryan agreed.

"Did you know Gina Hedlidge?"

"Who?" Bryan asked, looking really confused.

"We'll take that as a no," Officer Kerry said, looking over to Officer Brent, who was eyeing Bryan up suspiciously.

"Are you guys talking about the girl whose body they found the other day?" Bryan asked. "No, I didn't know her," he confirmed.

"Did you have any contact with her at all? Because someone described you to a tee as being the guy who was dancing with Gina that night. Is that true?" Officer Brent pushed.

"No, that's not true at all," Bryan said defensively.

"Can this Jocelyn confirm this?"

"Unfortunately, no. Jocelyn never showed up at the fair, but as I was leaving the fair, she texted me and asked me to meet her at her place. She said she had fallen asleep and apologized for not meeting me at the fair and she wanted to, um, make it up to me." Bryan smirked.

"How did she make it up to you?" Officer Kerry asked, being a bit of a prick.

"You know," Bryan said, smiling.

"No. Actually we don't know. Please tell us," Officer Kerry pressed.

"We had sex at her place," Bryan said, a little embarrassed.

"So Jocelyn can corroborate this story?" Officer Kerry asked, looking at Bryan to see if he could read his body language as he responded.

"Yes, she can," Bryan reassured the officers. "Am I under arrest?" he asked.

"No, not at all, you're free to leave whenever you want to," Officer Brent said, gesturing to the door.

Not impressed with his sarcastic attitude, Bryan walked toward the door, and when he opened it, he turned around and thanked the officers and said he hoped they would find the horrible person who did this terrible thing to that girl.

CHAPTER 62

Jocelyn

The loud, stern knock at the door startled Jocelyn. What surprised her even more were the two police officers standing on the opposite side of the door when she opened it.

"Jocelyn?" Officer Kelly asked.

"Yes," she responded nervously. "Come in, sit down. Would either of you like anything to drink?"

"No, thank you," both officers replied.

"We'd like to talk to you about last week, specifically last Wednesday night, when you were supposed to meet up with Bryan Mills."

"Bryan told us the two of you were supposed to meet up at the Silver Tree Acres fair, but that you didn't make it, so he came to you and the two of you had sex here at your place. Is that true?"

"Um," Jocelyn paused before responding, "yes, that's true. He was here. Why do you ask?"

"We are investigating the murder of Gina Hedlidge. Did you know her, or even know of her?"

"No."

"Has Bryan ever brought up the name Gina?"

"No. Never."

"Does Bryan have any violent tendencies?"

"Not that I'm aware of."

"What time did Bryan come here on Wednesday night after he left the fair?"

"I think it was, like, ten."

185

"You think it was ten?" Officer Brent repeated, raising his eyebrows.

"It was ten. I'm sure of it. It was ten o' clock," Jocelyn reiterated.

"Did Bryan appear shaken up or disgruntled in any way?"

"No, not at all."

"Okay, well, that's all the questions we have for now. May we contact you down the road if we have any further questions or concerns?"

"Absolutely," Jocelyn replied.

"Well, thank you for your time, ma'am." The officers tipped their hats and let themselves out the front door.

CHAPTER 63

Lena

I waited outside of Frederick's for Bryan for about ten minutes, then walked back inside to wait for another ten minutes, as the wind was brisk, but Bryan never showed.

Odd, I thought. I decided just to brave the chill in the air and head home alone. Maybe Bryan was asked to stay late, or maybe he went home sick. *You would think he would have called me, but maybe he just got really busy and forgot. So unlike him, though.*

When I walked through our front door, I noticed Chance sitting on the couch, but no Bryan in sight.

Just as I was about to ask Chance if he had heard from Bryan, the front door swung open, and in he stepped. The front door slammed closed, but by the surprised look on Bryan's face, I didn't think it was intentional.

"You'll never believe what just happened to me," Bryan blurted out. "Lena, I'm so sorry I didn't make it to pick you up from work, but just as I stepped foot out of Constantine's, two officers approached me—"

Before Bryan could finish his sentence, Chance chimed in, "You too?"

"Wait, were you questioned too?" Bryan asked.

"Yes. That's why I wasn't home for dinner last night. That's also why I blew you guys off this morning when I said I didn't want to talk about it. I was embarrassed. Sorry about that, I honestly wasn't sure how to handle the situation. Two officers came to the front door and said they needed to ask me some questions. Not comfortable

187

with the officers coming into the house, I offered to follow them down to the station.

"They asked me a bunch of questions about that girl, Gina, that was killed last Wednesday, the night of the fair. They said someone described me as being the guy who was talking to her that night."

"No way!" Bryan jumped in. "That's the same bullshit they just said to me. I'd love to know who those informants were, because they clearly need their eyes checked. Did you know her?" he asked Chance.

"No, but I think she may be related to one of the dancers I work with. That would be the extent of me 'knowing her,'" Chance said, using air quotes.

"So let me get this straight, both of you were persons of interest in the murder that just took place?" I asked. I knew they both could hear the worry in my voice from the expressions on their faces.

"Lena, you have nothing to worry about. Neither Chance nor I would ever do anything like that. Come on, you know us," Bryan pleaded.

It took me a couple of seconds before I responded, "I know, I know."

It was a very, very quiet dinner that night.

CHAPTER 64

Chance

"Leeza, I'm so nervous. I was questioned yesterday by two officers about a murder that took place last Wednesday night at the town fair here," Chance said, sounding extremely anxious.

"Did you do anything wrong?" Leeza asked, already knowing what the answer would be.

"Of course not, but my concern is, what if the cops start digging into my past and find out about what happened with Amanda? And if they find out that I'm a wanted man in Cloverfield, Maine, they will totally try to pin this on me, no doubt."

"Chance, relax. If you didn't do anything wrong, then you have nothing to worry about. Just continue with your life like nothing ever happened. Don't let this get you down. You have had enough drama as it is. Keep your head up. Stay strong."

Before Chance could even say another word, Leeza said, "I have to run," and quickly hung up the phone.

———

Chance was really feeling down and depressed due to the current situation. He knew Bryan really cared about Lena, but he himself was not currently caring so much about Bryan's feelings. He selfishly wanted to spend some alone time with Lena. *What if I really do get arrested?* he thought. So he went ahead and texted Lena, not giving it a second thought, "Hi, Lena, was wondering if you and I could go out for some dinner later. Just the two of us."

Then he waited.

CHAPTER 65

Lena

I was on my lunch break, sitting in the small cramped break room in the back of Frederick's, when my phone buzzed. I read the text message from Chance about going out to dinner but decided not to respond right away. Instead, I just placed my phone back in my back pants pocket.

"Lena, is everything okay?" Margie asked with concern in her voice.

"Hey, Margie. Yes, I'm okay, just feeling a little down and out. I am in desperate need of a girls' night out. It feels like it's been forever," I said with a heavy sigh.

"You want to go grab a couple of drinks later?"

"You know, Margie, I think I'd really like that. I'm going to take you up on that offer," I replied, smiling as I got ready to walk back out onto the floor.

I pulled my phone out of my back pocket and texted Chance back, "Sorry but I already have plans."

I hit send, placed the phone in my back pocket, and back to work I went.

CHAPTER 66

Chance

Chance heard his phone *ping*. He quickly grabbed it, and when he looked down at the screen, he frowned. "So much for that," he quietly mumbled to himself.

Then he got an idea, which perked him up.

I'm going to take the night off and surprise Lena with some flowers when she gets home from work.

Chance grabbed his jacket, threw it on, and shuffled out the door.

CHAPTER 67

Jocelyn

Jocelyn peered around the work floor at Constantine's until she found what she was looking for then quickly approached.

"Bryan, what happened yesterday?" Jocelyn asked, acting surprised. She didn't want to tell him about the officers coming to her house or that she had lied to them about Bryan being with her the night of the murder.

Someday she would reveal what she did for him, in a future effort to bring the two of them closer together.

"The cops just asked me some questions about where I was and what I did Wednesday night, the night of the Silver Tree Acres fair. The officers said that someone told them they thought they saw me there that night with the woman who was murdered."

"Were you?"

"Gosh, no. They questioned Chance, too, saying the exact same thing."

Jocelyn was so tempted to ask him where he really was that night of the murder. Although she told the officers that her and Bryan were at her place having sex that evening, she knew that was far from the truth. She would have been in her glory if that was what really took place that night, that's for sure. She had been waiting to get her claws into him.

She decided to let it go, for now. She didn't want to upset the man she hoped someday would ask her to marry him.

Chapter 68

Lena

Bryan appeared to be in a peppy mood on our way home from work, chatting up a storm.

That was until I told him I'd be going out with Margie for a few drinks at Peeves tonight, after dinner. It was as if Bryan's entire demeanor changed. He suddenly had this blank stare. Then he calmly said, "That's nice," and didn't say another word afterward.

When we walked through the front door, Bryan went straight up the stairs to his room and closed the door. *Weird*, I thought.

Chance came out of his room to greet me before I retreated to the upstairs as well.

"Hey, I'm sorry about not being able to go out to dinner with you tonight," I said, but in all honesty I didn't feel guilt-ridden.

Chance just smiled and said, "It's okay. Maybe we can do it another day?"

Oh, those damn eyes. So hard to stay mad at!

"Sure." I didn't have the heart to say no. I just really needed this one day to myself. "I have to go get ready," I said, hoping Chance wouldn't think I was trying to avoid him.

I genuinely just wanted to go get ready and leave.

"Right, okay," he said, putting his hands in the air like he was throwing in the towel, then turned and walked away.

When I came back downstairs after getting ready, Chance was sitting at the dining room table looking defeated.

"I hope you have fun tonight, Lena. Please be careful out there." Then he offered, "Do you want me to at least drop you off at Peeves?"

Chance saying "Be careful out there" kind of creeped me out. I know I was being foolish, but considering the recent events that just took place, I really couldn't blame myself for thinking that way.

"Chance, I appreciate the offer, but I'll be fine, thanks." Seeing the disappointment on his face, I had to think fast. "Oh, look at that," I said, looking down at my phone. "Margie just texted me and said she's going to meet me halfway to Peeves so her and I can walk together," I lied, walking quickly toward the front door.

On the walk to Peeves, a million and one things ran through my head. I probably should have been terrified to be walking alone outside, but for some strange reason I wasn't.

Chapter 69

Lena

Peeves had the usual crowd. Not too many patrons since it wasn't yet the weekend. The crowd was actually pretty decent for a Wednesday, though.

About an hour and a half and five beers later, I was feeling pretty good. I could tell Margie was feeling it as well. We chatted and laughed about work and life itself. I didn't dare tell her about Chance or Bryan being questioned about the murder that happened at the Silver Tree Acres fair. I wasn't sure what she'd think. Hell, I didn't even know what I thought about the situation.

Then just as Margie asked me about my living arrangements with Chance and Bryan, Chance walked into Peeves holding a bouquet of flowers.

"I hope you're not mad that I showed up here. I meant to give these to you earlier, but you left in such a hurry I forgot all about them, and I didn't want them to become wilted before you even had a chance to see them," Chance said, handing the flowers to me.

If I hadn't been drinking, my reaction may have gone a little differently, but I was feeling no pain and surprisingly was a little excited to see him. So instead of yelling at him or telling him to leave, I told him to pull up a chair and join us.

"Wait, shouldn't you be at work?" I asked in somewhat of a drunken slur.

"I took the night off," he replied, taking a swig of his beer.

"Let's cheers to that!" I said, clinking my bottle against his and Margie's.

"I'll be right back, you two. Don't do anything I would do," Margie said, smirking walking toward the ladies' room.

When Margie arrived back at the table, Chance and I had just finished doing another shot of tequila.

"Oh boy, the two of you are going to be wasted," Margie said, laughing.

"Oh, and like you're not," I said, giving Margie a "just messin' with ya" kind of look.

Chance is looking really good. Extra sexy. Not sure if this is the alcohol talking. Probably. I feel like I want to lick him. That sounds strange, I thought to myself, then suddenly, I was brought back to reality when Margie slapped my arm.

"Well, do you?" Margie asked.

"Do I what?" I asked.

"Come on, just one game." Margie laughed. It wasn't until she started walking toward the dartboard that I realized what she had asked me.

"Darts! Yes!" I agreed. "I'm not too good at darts, so keep your distance from the dartboard. Sadly, I have terrible aim and may hit you by accident, so just stay clear." I laughed, hoping that I didn't slur my words.

Margie went first and of course got a bull's-eye on the first throw. When it was my turn, the first dart I threw bounced off the board and landed at Chance's feet. I just looked over and smiled. I could feel my face turning red from embarrassment.

As I got into position to throw the next dart, I felt the heat of another body up against me. Then I could feel hands slide around my waist, and one grabbed my right hand, the one I throw the darts with.

Chance whispered in my ear to steady myself, then to aim, and we threw the dart together. I actually made it onto the board. I was so excited I jumped around and yelled like I had just won the freaking lottery. Thankfully, there were only a few patrons left in the bar.

When we wrapped up our last dart game, Margie called it a night. Chance and I thought it was best we head home too, but not before doing one last shot together.

"Lena," Chance said drunkenly. "I really like you. Like really, really like you, but I know you and Bryan kind of have—"

"Kind of have what?" I asked, rudely cutting him off.

"Well, you know."

"No, Chance, I don't know. Please do tell," I said, running my hand through his hair. I felt that warm, amazing feeling slowly trickling up my body. I was horny. I wanted to have him right then and there.

Just then Chance leaned in and kissed me. Our lips connected, and his tongue made its way into my mouth. He cradled my head between his hands. We were so in the moment I almost forgot we were in a public place.

"Let's continue this back at our place," Chance said softly, looking directly into my eyes. I responded by just smiling back at him. I sat down in the passenger seat of Chance's rusty orange sedan, and out of nowhere Bryan popped into my mind, making me shudder.

"Hey, I have an idea. Just in case Bryan is home, why don't we go to the old barn behind my house. I haven't been in the barn in a really long time, but I'm sure there is still hay in there." I chuckled. "It won't be as comfortable as a bed, but it'll do the job," I said, smirking.

CHAPTER 70

Lena

We pulled up to the front of the house and saw that Bryan's truck was there. Chance shut the engine off, and as quietly as we could, we got out and shut the doors slowly in an attempt not to wake Bryan if he was sleeping.

"So what's the story about this barn? Did it used to hold livestock?"

"It did at one time. My father and I used to feed the animals together every day." My insides tingled when Chance asked me personal questions. It made me feel like he really cared about me and my feelings. As if he was truly interested in getting to know me.

Together, Chance and I gently pulled open one of the barn doors, hoping that it wouldn't make any noise. To our luck, it didn't!

Once we were inside the barn, I began telling Chance about my childhood: how I helped milk the cows and collect the eggs from the chickens, brush the horses, and feed the pigs.

Then without a warning, this awful smell hit us.

"It smells kind of funny in here, doesn't it?" I asked, scrunching my nose.

"It definitely has a strange smell, but it's not going to keep me from doing this."

Chance reached out and grabbed my face and began kissing me passionately. A continuation from the bar. He lifted my shirt up and over my head and arms and unclipped my bra, completely exposing my breasts. I could feel my nipples harden up from the brisk air. His mouth left my lips and slowly traveled down my neck, to my breasts,

199

where he tickled my nipples with his tongue, and then engulfed one breast at a time in his mouth. It felt amazing.

While he was busy making out with my breasts, I reached down to unbuckle his pants and maneuver them down his legs. First with my hands and then the rest of the way with my feet. He, too, was tugging at my pants, but with them being skinny jeans, they were practically suctioned to my body, so we both had to work together to get them off.

It was so dark in the barn it was hard to see much of any-thing, but we could definitely feel all of each other. We both stood there stark naked, exploring each other's body through touch. Then Chance put both of his hands under my butt cheeks, lifted me up so that my legs would wrap around his waist, and gently laid me down onto the somewhat-soft straw. Then we were skin to skin as he laid on top of me.

My extreme excitement allowed him to enter me with ease. He definitely didn't disappoint. But while our sweaty bodies were locked together, there was a loud thud, which made me practically jump up from under Chance.

We stayed very still, just listening.

"What do you think that was?" I whispered, sounding like a frightened child.

"It sounded like the barn door opened and shut, but we would have seen someone enter if someone came in because we are right next to the door," Chance whispered with a nervous chuckle.

"Not to freak you out, but there's another set of doors at the other end of the barn," I said.

Chance was quiet for a moment and then said, "Fuck it," and we continued with our lovemaking.

CHAPTER 71

Jocelyn

The knocking at the door frightened Jocelyn from her sleep.

"I'm coming," she said in a groggy voice, making her way toward the front door.

"Hey," she said, alarmed, combing her fingers through her hair, trying to fix it.

"I'm sorry, did I wake you?"

"No, I was just lying on the couch watching television, that's all. Come in!" she said, making a welcoming hand gesture. "Make yourself at home. Sorry, my house is a little messy, I wasn't expecting any guests," she said with a nervous giggle as he walked right past her as if she wasn't even there.

"You said you were watching television? Why's the television off then?" he asked, walking around glancing at stuff like he was looking for something specific.

"I quickly turned it off when I heard the rap at the door. Do you know it's midnight?" she asked, not even realizing how late it was until she looked up at the clock hanging on her kitchen wall.

"You have some nice digs," he said, making it sound like he was surprised that she had a nice home, completely ignoring her question about the time.

"Are you all right?" Jocelyn asked nervously. "You're acting strange."

She started following him throughout her house. When they reached her bedroom, he grabbed her face and began kissing her. Hard. Jocelyn's fears and worries melted away as she kissed him. She felt safe. She had patiently waited for this moment, and it was finally happening. She was enjoying every second of it. Suddenly he grabbed her by the waist and threw her on the bed. "You are one of those boys that like it rough, aren't you?" Jocelyn asked, smiling.

He didn't answer her. He just continued by lifting her night-gown up and ripping her panties off. He stripped down until he was completely naked too. Then he lifted her nightgown up and over her head, but instead of taking it off, he just left it over her face.

There was no foreplay. Not that she needed it, so he just crawled up on her and jammed himself into her hard and fast. She let out a scream of pleasure and pain at the same time. He put his hands around her neck and proceeded to squeeze a little bit harder every time he jammed himself inside of her.

She clawed at his hands around her neck until her arms eventually just went limp. He climaxed, ejaculating inside of her, slowly releasing his hands from her neck.

As he began dressing himself, he heard Jocelyn take in a gulp of air then start coughing.

"What the fuck!" she screamed directly at him. "Next time, can you give me a heads-up that you're going to choke me during sex? I don't care if that's what gets you off, but you have to at least let me know ahead of time. My god, you scared the shit out of me."

He whispered "Sorry" under his breath, but he continued putting his shoes on and walked right toward the door to leave.

"Can we do this again?" Jocelyn pleaded.

He stopped in his tracks, and with his head looking down at the floor, he mumbled, "This shouldn't have happened."

"Come again?" Jocelyn said, not able to clearly hear what he said.

He didn't repeat himself, just continued to walk out of her front door.

When he got into his truck, he beat on the steering wheel screaming. "Why? Why'd she have to do this? What's wrong with me? Why can't she just love me?"

CHAPTER 72

Lena

"Here, let me turn my phone light on so that we can find our clothes," Chance offered.

As he shone his light upon the hay, I noticed a dark red spot close by us. At first, I thought it might be a shadow from one of us, but I leaned closer and realized it wasn't.

"Oh my god, Chance, is that blood?" I asked, backing up.

I was hoping he'd say no, but instead he said just the opposite and agreed with me. "It definitely looks like dried-up blood," as he moved his phone light across what appeared to be a trail of it leading toward the other end of the barn.

"Maybe it's from a wounded animal," I suggested. "Maybe that was what we heard earlier."

"That would've had to be one large animal, because this is a lot of blood," Chance shot back.

"You don't think it's from a person, do you?" I asked nervously.

"Honestly, I'm not sure, and I really don't want to find out. So can we grab our stuff and get the hell out of here?" Chance asked, with the sound of fear in his voice.

"We never locked the barn after we sold all of our livestock, so literally anybody could…I can't even say it. I think I'm going to be…" Sure enough, I vomited right in front of this gorgeous human being, and God only knows what he was thinking.

"Hey, take it easy," Chance said, rubbing my back. "We don't even know for sure that it came from a human being."

"Why are you so calm about this?" Then right after asking that question, it hit me like a ton of bricks, the reason I went out in the first place. Both guys were questioned about the murder of a girl at the fair. Were each of them considered suspects? A chill ran up my spine, and I felt like I was going to throw up again. Feeling nervous and scared, I held my hand over my mouth and ran out of the barn toward the house in my bra and underwear, clutching my clothes with my free hand.

Chance yelled out behind me, "Lena! Seriously! You know I'd never do anything to hurt anyone! Lena, please stop!"

I didn't stop.

"Fuck!" he yelled out loud.

Bryan must have been sitting on the couch and jumped up when he heard me run through the front door. He ran straight toward me when I entered the house, as did Chewie.

"Lena, is everything okay? Oh my god, where are your clothes? Did somebody hurt you? I will kill them!" Bryan growled.

I couldn't answer him as I needed to make it to the bathroom. The hand over my mouth could only hold the vomit back for so long.

I ran straight up the stairs, right to the toilet without closing the door, with Chewie following right behind me. I could hear a scuffle downstairs.

"You motherfucker, what'd you do to her, you fucking asshole!" Bryan said screaming directly at Chance. Then Bryan took a swing and hit Chance right in the nose. Not even two seconds later his nose began gushing blood. With all his force, Chance pummeled Bryan. The two of them struggled to gain control over each other, but continuously losing their grip as they slipped on the blood that fell from Chance's nose all over the floor.

"Stop it!" I screamed at the top of my lungs walking down the stairs. Both guys let go of one another and looked up at me.

"Lena, what the fuck? Why are you half-naked, and why does this bozo here have his shirt off? Did he hurt you? Did he force himself on you?" Bryan raged.

"Bryan, stop! I'm tired, stressed, and scared. Let's all go to bed. We'll discuss all of this in the morning."

"Lena, but—" Chance began, but I cut him off.

"Chance, please, just go to bed. I need time to think," I said, holding my hand in the air.

I turned, walked into my room, and slammed the door shut. I could still hear them bickering back and forth until I finally heard Chance's bedroom door slam shut as well.

Then there was a soft tapping on my door.

"Lena? Are you sure you're okay?" Bryan asked in a soft tone.

"Yes, Bryan. I'm fine. Please just leave me alone right now," I grumbled.

Then I could hear him slowly retreat to his room and close the door.

CHAPTER 73

Bryan

Oh, man, this is perfect! Lena's pissed off at Chance, and although I'm not sure what for, this could be my opportunity to jump in and be the hero and save the day! Bryan thought to himself with a huge smile on his face as he fell asleep.

Lena

Bryan must have woken up and come downstairs just before I did. He'd started the hot water for coffee and tea by the time I entered the kitchen, and I think he could tell by the look on my face that something was bothering me.

"Lena, are you sure you're okay? Do you want to talk?"

"Actually, I'm not okay," I whispered, hopefully low enough that Chance wouldn't hear me.

"Chance and I, we went into the barn last night—"

Before I could finish my sentence, Bryan blurted out, "You two were in the barn?"

His reaction startled me, and then he asked the dreaded question, "What were the two of you doing in the barn together? Actually, no," Bryan said, holding up his hand. "Never mind, please don't answer that. I honestly don't want to know."

Trying to respect Bryan's wishes, I tried to explain the evening without going into too much detail. "When I left Peeves, I ran into Chance, and we decided to walk around, and we just strolled into the barn and in order for us to see where, um, we, um, were walking, Chance used the light from his cell phone to shine at our feet, and there was, there was…"

"There was what, Lena? What?" Bryan urged.

"Blood, Bryan! There was blood all over the hay!"

"So you're telling me that you and Chance just decided to stroll into the barn together—"

"Bryan, did you not just hear what I said? There was blood! Blood, Bryan, blood!"

"I heard you. That's crazy! How do you think it got there? Oh my god, do you think Chance has something to do with it? Is that why you were running away from him last night? I kind of feel like Sherlock Holmes," Bryan joked.

"This isn't a laughing matter, Bryan!" I said, disgusted.

As Bryan and I whispered back and forth, Chewie just sat between the two of us looking up at me, then at Bryan, wagging his tail.

"Well, I have something to show you," Bryan began. "Just don't get mad at me for doing this. Please. I found something out about Chance."

Chewie barked and moved away from us.

"Chance, good morning!" we said in unison. "You're up early."

"Yeah, I didn't sleep very much last night. Why were you guys whispering?" Chance asked, yawning, sounding a little confused.

"We didn't want to wake you, is all," I said, lying through my teeth.

"Oh, well, that was nice of the two of you. Hey, Lena, could you and I talk for a moment?" Chance asked nicely.

"Actually, we have to leave soon. I told Margie I'd come in a little early to help stock shelves before the store opens," I replied, lying once again.

"Okay. Can we chat later when you get out of work?" Chance asked, sounding a bit annoyed.

"Sure. We can do that." As soon as I said those words, I looked directly at Bryan, and without me saying a word, he knew the look of, "I don't want to be alone with this man."

When Bryan and I hopped into his truck and shut the doors, Bryan suddenly blurted out, "Okay, since we have a few extra minutes, can we go somewhere and talk?"

"Sure," I responded, feeling kind of nervous, not sure what to expect.

"So," Bryan began, "I decided to Google the name Chance Wallace, and you'll never believe what I found!" But before he could continue, my phone rang. It was my dad. I had to answer it or he would worry, I hadn't talked to him in days.

"Morning, Daddy!"

"How's my little muffin doing?" he asked.

"I'm great! Bryan and I are on our way to work. How's everything in Florida?"

"Sweetie, it's awesome. I'm so glad I moved here. So listen, the reason I'm actually calling you is because I wanted to fly you down here. There's someone here that I would like you to meet!"

I paused, not really sure what to say. "You mean like a girlfriend or something?" I asked, trying not to sound too unenthusiastic.

"Yes, actually! Her name is Addie. I really think you're going to like her. She can't wait to meet you."

I wasn't sure how to respond, so I just sat there silently.

"How's Bryan doing?" Dad inquired.

"He's great. He's actually right here next to me." I put my phone on speaker, not anticipating what my dad was about to say next.

"Bring Bryan along with you! It'd be so great to see him. I assume there are no wedding bells yet in the near future since I haven't received any exciting phone calls from you yet," my dad said jokingly.

"Hi, Mr. McAnderson! I'd love to come visit you," Bryan said, looking directly at me.

"Hey, son, how are you doing?" My dad sounded excited to hear Bryan's voice.

"I'm doing awesome, in part since I'm living with and taking care of your lovely daughter. And by the way, I'd take your daughter's hand any day if she'd let me!" Bryan said, smiling at me.

"Yeah, okay, enough of that," I said, breaking the awkward stare between Bryan and me. "We have to run, Dad, thanks for calling and checking in. Love you! We'll talk soon." I made a smooching sound before ending the call.

Embarrassed, I quickly grabbed the door handle and jumped out of the truck heading toward the front doors of Frederick's.

Feeling guilty for the abrupt escape, I turned around and headed back toward Bryan's truck, just as he was about to pull away and still had the look of "What the hell just happened?" on his face.

He rolled his window down as I approached.

"Did you really mean that, Bryan?" I asked softly.

He looked directly into my eyes before responding, "Yes, Lena. I really meant that."

Then with a sad look on his face, he slowly drove away.

CHAPTER 74

Jocelyn

"Good morning, Bryan!" Jocelyn said, sounding giddy as he walked through the front door.

"Good morning, Jocelyn," Bryan responded, but with very little enthusiasm.

Walking beside him, she leaned in and whispered, "Last night was the best fuck I ever had, Mr. Mills! When can we do it again? I am super wet right now just thinking about it." She licked his earlobe.

Unexpectedly, Jocelyn grabbed Bryan and dragged him into the women's bathroom. She threw the cleaning sign outside the door, hoping no one would walk in. She pushed Bryan into the handicapped stall, locking the door. She unzipped his pants and pulled out his penis, stroking it a few times before lifting up her skirt and removing her panties. She wrapped her left leg around his body before placing herself up on him.

Bryan just stood there with no emotion, but it felt so damn good. So he closed his eyes and envisioned that it was Lena.

"I knew you would enjoy this," Jocelyn whispered in his ear between groans.

"Please be quiet," Bryan whispered back.

Not sure she heard him correctly, she continued, "I knew someday you'd come around. You're mine, Bryan Mills!" she said, breathing heavily.

Just then Bryan grabbed her by the hair, swung her around so that her right cheek was flush with the wall, and began fucking her hard and fast.

"Bryan, this is a little rough."

He pushed her face back up against the wall and said, "I told you to shut the fuck up!" Then he leaned in close to her ear and as he released himself inside of her, he whispered, "We'll never be together! I just asked Lena to marry me!"

Jocelyn quickly turned around and shoved Bryan as hard as she could against the opposite side of the bathroom stall wall. "You fucking asshole! How dare you!" she growled at him.

"Don't get mad at me. You started this," Bryan said, buttoning his shirt and smirking.

Jocelyn was so angry she slapped him across the face and stormed out of the bathroom, still in the midst of adjusting her clothes.

Bryan chuckled softly to himself before exiting the bathroom.

CHAPTER 75

Lena

It was such a nice day outside that Sandy and I decided to eat our lunch outside at the small black iron picnic table that sat right next to Frederick's front doors.

When we sat down at the picnic bench, we could hear arguing in the distance. The sun was bright, so it was a bit hard to see, but when I covered my eyes with my hand and looked in the direction of Constantine's, I noticed Bryan and Jocelyn yelling at each other.

That's odd, I thought. Curiosity got the best of me, and I told Sandy I'd be right back. I began to walk toward Bryan and Jocelyn. Jocelyn also appeared to be walking directly toward me, but then Bryan grabbed her by the arm and said something into her ear. She looked angry at whatever he had just said to her. Then she turned and walked through the front doors of Constantine's just as I arrived.

"Is everything okay?" I asked Bryan. "It looked like the two of you were arguing about something."

"Me and Jocelyn?" Bryan laughed. "No, no, no, we were just talking about work. She was just letting off some steam about stuff she hates about this place. That's all. No biggie."

"It looked as if she was walking right towards me, though, before you grabbed her arm and said something to her."

"Oh, that! No, she wanted to bitch to you about her troubles at work, and I told her not to bother you with that stuff as you had enough going on in your life right now and that you didn't need any more stress added to it. Especially hers!"

"Ah, I see! Well, thank you, because to be honest with you, I'm not really a big fan of hers. Okay then, since everything is all good, enjoy the rest of your lunch break, and I'll see you at five." I waved as I walked away.

"Sounds good to me," Bryan said, waving back at me before turning and entering the building, scowling.

Little did I know, I missed the darkness that overcame Bryan as I turned and walked away. His smile faded, and his eyes turned dark. Had I known what that conversation between him and Jocelyn was actually about, maybe it would have saved the next few incidents from happening.

I apparently missed what truly transpired.

CHAPTER 76

Jocelyn

"Hey, look who's walking right this way! Perfect timing!" Jocelyn yelled at Bryan as she saw me get up from the picnic table.

"Jocelyn, you better rethink your actions," Bryan warned her. "She will not believe you anyway," he snapped.

"Well, let's see what she has to say about it," Jocelyn threatened.

Bryan grabbed her by the arm to keep her from walking toward Lena.

"Ouch, Bryan, you're hurting me! Let go!" Jocelyn whimpered.

"If you don't want to endure any further pain, you better go inside this building right now before she gets here, or you'll end up like that girl at the fair."

"Yeah, right." Jocelyn laughed until she saw the blank stare in Bryan's eyes. It was like she was looking at a completely different person.

"Leave. Right. Now," he warned her again. "Or there'll be unfortunate consequences. Trust me!"

Jocelyn, sensing now that Bryan was not joking around, turned and walked through the front doors of Constantine's, right before Lena had approached.

CHAPTER 77

Lena

I sat alone in the quiet house. The boys were out and about, except for Chewie. I started to think about Becca's wedding. It was right around the corner. I needed to start packing. I started to think that maybe Bryan wasn't the right person to take to Becca's wedding, but at the moment I didn't trust Chance. Although, he would be great eye candy and wonderful to show off.

Bryan, well, he seemed off lately, withdrawn. Not himself.

My heart is telling me Bryan, but my instincts are telling me Chance. Just when I finished that thought, Chance walked through the front door.

Chance

"Hi, Lena, I need to get ready and go to work, but I just want to say I'm sorry about all of this. I'm not a killer. I'd never hurt you. What's in that barn is not my doing. I do understand though that you are freaked out and confused, so I'm going to leave you alone. I'm not going to press you if you're not ready to talk. If you decide that you want me to move out, just let me know. I probably should've never moved in in the first place. Let me know if you want me to leave, and I'll start packing my stuff tomorrow." Chance sounded sad.

"Chance, stop. I jumped to conclusions. Yes, it has freaked me out for sure, and yes, I'm confused, but I honestly don't think you killed anyone. I just need some time to think things through and gather my thoughts. Don't go. Well, I mean, go to work, but you don't need to move out. Just give me a little time to process every-thing. I don't think you are capable of murder, but I do feel that there is something you are hiding, and if there is something you are hiding, it'd be best to tell me before I find out some other way."

"I have nothing to hide from you, Lena, besides the fact that I may be in love with you."

"Oh" was all that emerged from my mouth.

I felt my face turn red. I really needed to keep my head on straight and be careful because Bryan had yet to tell me something important about Chance.

Feeling a little awkward, I turned away from Chance and walked up to my room. I plopped down on my bed, and right beside me was Chewie, waiting patiently to give me lots of kisses.

CHAPTER 78

Lena

I could hear Chance's footsteps downstairs, then about ten minutes later I heard the front door open and close.

I looked at Chewie and asked, "How'd things get so complicated?" My response from Chewie was a sideways tilt of the head. "You're so lucky to be a dog. No worries in the world. Except, of course, when you have to use the bathroom, and no one is home to let you out. That has to be really rough!" Again, Chewie's response was another sideways tilt of the head.

The knocking at the front door was unexpected. Before I could even ask Chewie who he thought it could be, he was already out of the bedroom and making his way down the stairs.

When I opened the front door, I was shocked to see Jocelyn standing there. She looked rough, like she had been crying. I almost felt bad for her, until she opened her mouth and started talking.

"I just wanted to let you know that Bryan and I have been sleeping together, and earlier today when you saw us arguing, it was because I wanted to tell you about us, but he didn't want me to. I screwed him at work today. He's a great fuck, which I bet you already knew, but he is mine, so I'm warning you to stay the fuck away from him. He doesn't want you! He loves me, I give him great head and allow him to do anything he wants with me. Anything he wants, I will do."

I was speechless and just stared at her. Not exactly sure how to respond.

"Hello! Did you hear me? Earth to Lena?" Jocelyn said in her high-pitched voice, waving her hands in front of my face.

Then I just snapped. "Get your skank ass the hell off of my porch, and don't you ever show your face here again," I said, then slammed the door in her face and locked it. I ran back up to my room, but before I even had a chance to process what just took place, I heard the front door open again.

CHAPTER 79

Lena

I walked out of my room to see Bryan walking through the front door with a bouquet of flowers in his hand, and when he looked up at me, a huge smile spread across his face.

I didn't even let him get a word in before going off.

"How dare you tell me that you want to marry me, with my father on the phone no less, then go to work and fuck Jocelyn! Wipe that stupid fucking look off your face! Your fuck buddy was just here and told me all about your rendezvous with her. I'm such a freaking idiot for thinking for a second that you really meant what you said."

"But, Lena—"

"Don't you 'But, Lena' me! I can't believe you slept with that bimbo. I really thought you cared about me." The tears started uncontrollably rolling down my face. My heart hurt. I wasn't sure what to do at that moment or even what to say.

"Lena, please," Bryan pleaded. "I do love you! I have loved you from the moment I laid eyes on you. You're all I ever think about. Jocelyn means absolutely nothing to me. Lena, I swear! I did sleep with her once, but that was because I was angry when you were out drinking with Chance. It meant nothing at all. You're the only person in this entire world that I care about. Words cannot even come close enough to describe the way I feel about you. I do want to marry you. I made a mistake. Please—" But before he could finish his sentence, I cut him off.

"First of all, you have a terrible way of showing that you care about someone. Second, what did you mean you were angry when I

219

was out drinking with Chance? How'd you know Chance and I were even drinking together? Were you spying on me?" The pitch of my voice got louder when I realized that Bryan would only know that information if he followed me out.

"I didn't say that," Bryan tried defending himself.

"Oh, yes, you did," I shot right back.

"I must've said that by accident. I didn't see—"

"Bryan, just stop! I don't want to hear any more bullshit come out from your mouth. Please go find somewhere else to sleep tonight. I'm sure your fuck buddy would be more than happy to let you stay at her place. I've nothing more to say to you. Please just go."

For the third time that day, I headed back into my room, Chewie by my side. I heard the front door open and close for the last time that day. My mind was spinning. I felt sick to my stomach. I felt like my entire world was crashing down on me.

I poured myself a glass of wine and washed some melatonin down with it.

Next thing I remember is waking up, and the sun was shining brightly through my window.

CHAPTER 80

Lena

When I walked out of my room into the hallway, the house was eerily quiet aside from Chewie prancing around. I peeked into Bryan's room to see if maybe he'd come back during the night, but his bed appeared that it hadn't been slept in. I honestly felt a little guilty that he really didn't come home.

Why'd that bitch ever have to come into the picture? I knew that there was no way that Bryan wouldn't be interested in her. I hate to admit it, but she's gorgeous. I'm just a small-town, country girl who still lives in the childhood house she grew up in, I scolded myself in my head as I made my cup of tea and sat by myself at the kitchen table in silence.

While I was getting dressed, the sun slowly faded away, and the sky turned dark, then rain began pelting angrily against the window, just like my mood.

My luck, of course! Oh! And I don't have a ride into work. Maybe the weather is giving me a sign that I should stay home today.

A crack of thunder made me jump and also helped me make up my mind about not walking in the crappy weather to work. So I called in.

I put my pajamas back on and crawled back into my nice, warm, cozy bed, where Chewie gladly joined me, and I fell fast asleep.

I woke up to a soft tapping on my bedroom door. When I said, "Come in," Chewie jumped off the bed and ran right to the door to greet Chance. Part of me hoped it would be Bryan.

"I hope I didn't wake you. I was looking for Chewie and noticed your bedroom door was closed. I wasn't sure if you were in here. I thought maybe Chewie wandered in and managed to shut the door and lock himself in. Is everything okay? Are you sick? Why are you home?" Chance asked, sounding concerned.

"I'm okay. I just needed a day off to clear my head, and why not call in on a gloomy, stormy day like today?" I said with my head squished against the pillow, with a half-smile on my face.

"Can I get you anything? Chance asked. He was standing in my bedroom doorway with no shirt on, wearing just some white nylon shorts that for some strange reason I couldn't seem to take my eyes off.

"Maybe a glass of water?" I suggested.

When Chance came over to the nightstand to set the glass of water down, I grabbed his arm and pulled him toward me. Part of me wanted him because he was sexy as hell, and the other part of me wanted to get back at Bryan for sleeping with that bitchy blonde.

"Kiss me," I said as I grabbed the back of his head and brought it toward me. We began making out, like it was our first time and we couldn't get enough of each other.

While we kissed, he pulled my tank top up over my head. His hands gently exploring, they felt so soft. His hands made their way to my panties, which were then pulled down and completely taken off.

Then he surprised me and went down on me. His tongue work was so amazing, he made me orgasm more than once. My body shook uncontrollably while this jolt ripped right up my body. It was the best feeling ever! He knew what he was doing down there for sure. *Hopefully not from practicing on the strippers—ew, ew, don't ruin this moment. Focus!* I scolded myself.

I had no clue that a woman could orgasm that many times in a row. Wow.

He then removed his shorts and joined me under the covers, laying his very tight, fit body over mine. He had no issues sliding right in. I was ready. He took it slow and was being gentle, which felt great, but I wanted more so I grabbed his butt and pulled him deeper inside me. It was painful yet pleasant.

I felt happy, but I also felt sad at the same time.

The thought of Bryan made me feel somewhat guilty. My mood quickly changed from excitement to feeling downright ashamed. Then sadly I couldn't wait for it to be over.

What the hell is wrong with me? I felt like a terrible person. I was so mad at Bryan, but at the same time I missed him. Then it was over.

CHAPTER 81

Bryan

Bryan woke up to the sun glaring in his eyes. As soon as he became more awake, the events of the night before came pummeling back at him. He quickly stood up and immediately began pacing back and forth, screaming at himself and smacking his hand against his head.

"Stupid, stupid, stupid. Why would she do that? Who does she think she is, just coming over and telling Lena about the two of us? Things weren't supposed to happen this way. Why can't Lena just understand that I love her and only her? Jocelyn means nothing to me at all! She just happened to be a free piece of ass at the times I was upset and needed someone. How do I fix this?" he asked himself.

He didn't get much of a good night sleep lying on the haystack, although it wasn't half bad, but a little chilly without a blanket. Where else was he going to go? He sure as hell didn't want to go to Jocelyn's house to spend the night. She was the whole reason he was in this mess in the first place.

He was pretty sure no one knew he'd slept in the barn. He hid his truck on the other side so that it was out of sight. He could see through the cracks of the barn that Chance was home.

He didn't see Lena leave the house. He wondered if maybe she had stayed home from work. He had called in this morning since he was still wearing the same clothes as yesterday and didn't have any clean clothes to change into.

As soon as he turned away from the barn door, he heard a car start. He instantly ran back to the barn door to see Chance's car pulling out. He could only make out one head, which meant that Lena, if she was home, she was home alone.

Should I go talk to her? Would she even talk to me? Maybe I should wait another day or two to let her cool off. She should hopefully be over it by then.

CHAPTER 82

Jocelyn

There was a knock at Jocelyn's door, and when she opened it, she was so excited to see him standing there. "Oh, hey, you! What brings you here, handsome? Come in, have a seat. Want some coffee?" Jocelyn asked, still in pink T-shirt and floral sweatpants.

"Today I decided I was just going to lounge around and be a bum," Jocelyn stammered. "I wasn't feeling work today. Do you ever have those days? Listen to me just chattering away. Sorry! So what brings you here today?"

"Jocelyn, I'm only going to ask this once, so please don't lie to me," he said, hoping she heard the hostility in his voice.

Jocelyn's smile disappeared from her face. "Okay."

"Did you go to my house the other day and say something that upset my roommate?"

"No, I don't know what you're talking about. Why in the world would I ever do something like that?"

"Jocelyn, I asked you to be honest with me," he reminded her.

"I'm being honest with you," she said, fidgeting. "Why would I lie about something like that?"

"Okay. Great. Would you like to go grab something to eat?" he asked, sounding more relaxed.

"I guess we could go grab some lunch," she responded nervously. "I just have to go get dressed."

"Okay, then go get dressed."

While Jocelyn was in her bedroom looking through her clothes in her closet, she turned around once and looked over her shoulder, as if she thought she sensed someone was behind her.

No one was there.

Then when she turned back toward the closet, suddenly there were hands around her neck, and they were tightening, constricting her airway. She lifted her hands up to try to loosen the grip, but she was weak and losing consciousness.

"I'm sorry, but you never had a chance," he said, letting her lifeless body fall to the floor.

CHAPTER 83

Lena

For it being a day off, it seemed to fly by so quickly. Before I knew it, the sun was beginning to set. Although it was late in the day, I decided to take a nice hot, steamy shower.

When I walked out of the bathroom with a soft white towel wrapped around my body and a soft pink towel wrapped around my head, singing softly to myself, Bryan was coming up the stairs.

"Oh my god! Bryan! You scared me!" I practically jumped out of my skin. Not because he was scary, I just hadn't heard him come in. Chewie came over to lick the excess water off my legs, with his rough bumpy tongue that felt like sandpaper.

"Hey, do you think we can talk after you get dressed?" Bryan asked.

"Sure, just give me a few minutes, and I'll meet you down-stairs," I replied, not making eye contact with him.

Just as I was about to close my door, Bryan asked, "Do you think we could pick out a movie and watch it together? You know, like the good old days?"

"Sure. Just like the good old days," I repeated with a smile on my face as I shut my bedroom door.

When I started down the stairs, I could hear popcorn popping and a disc being put into the DVD player. *I wonder what he picked out.*

When I got to the bottom of the stairs, Bryan rushed past me to go get the popcorn and pop from the kitchen. "Go sit down," he said in passing.

When Bryan came back into the living room, he set the popcorn on the table next to the couch, grabbed both of my hands to pull me up off the couch, then sat down and tugged at my hand to sit with him, between his legs, so we could cuddle. *Odd, I thought considering we hadn't talked yet about the other night.*

The popcorn was at a perfect distance that Bryan and I could easily reach. Chewie jumped up on the couch to join us.

The Cabin in the Woods started to play.

"Yes!" I yelled, putting both arms up in the air. "Chris Hemsworth!" We both started laughing at my crazy outburst. For the first time in a while, it truly did feel like old times, before any of the drama. I wished we could turn back time and start all over again.

What I did next, though, I didn't really put much thought into it before doing it, and it was just really bad timing on my part.

CHAPTER 84

Lena

When the movie ended, I got up from between Bryan's legs and turned around to face him.

"So I think I changed my mind about who I'm going to take as my plus-one to Becca's wedding." I honestly was extremely nervous about his reaction since we'd just had that falling-out.

The smile immediately fell from Bryan's face, and I felt for a second that I was looking into the eyes of the devil himself. His entire demeanor changed. I felt scared. I was frozen with fear.

Bryan slowly got up off the couch. "Wow, so you decided to take him over me, huh?" He started pacing back in forth in front of the couch with his head down. "Guess I no longer need that tux I already wasted my money on. Might as well throw that right down the shitter."

"I'm so sorry, Bryan," I said, reaching my arm out toward him.

He startled me by screaming, "Don't touch me!"

"I just thought Chance really has no one here, and you, well, you have at least Jocelyn to hang out with."

He stopped pacing and looked up at me with a look of death upon his face. Something was not right. I could feel it. His face was bright red.

"Please tell me you're joking," he said, looking straight into my eyes, but before I could even respond, he yelled, "She is fucking dead! Dead! Dead! Dead!"

"What?" I screamed, horrified.

"I said she is dead…to me," he said, but much quieter this time. He held his hand over his heart like it was broken. Then the tears started to fall, and he dropped to his knees.

I felt like I needed to console him, but at the same time I was feeling really scared. I could swear I had just witnessed three different people come out of the same person.

Not sure what to say or do, I apologized again, went to my room, and locked the door. I quickly changed my clothes and went back downstairs but headed straight for the front door, hoping he was not going to try to stop me.

I felt so bad for making Bryan feel this way.

When he yelled that Jocelyn was dead, I really thought he meant she was actually, well, dead.

How foolish of me, Bryan couldn't even hurt a fly if he tried, I laughed to myself. I took a deep breath in and tried to shake off the eerie feeling that I had.

CHAPTER 85

Lena

I walked and walked until I found myself at the front doors of Wesley's strip club. I had to convince myself to actually walk through the doors. I really wasn't sure what to expect.

Finally I just grabbed the handle, swung the door open, and walked in like I owned the place. That was until I noticed all the beautiful topless women who were crackhead skinny. Then I cowered down a bit.

"Lena?"

I turned my head to the right to see Chance behind the bar, making cocktails for a group of men and a hot blonde leaning over with her boobs laying on the bar and her ass sticking out. It appeared there was only a lacy pink triangle above her butt cheeks, so my guess was she had a thong on. *Talk about leaving absolutely nothing to the imagination! Except for her vajayjay.*

After the blond chick and the men walked away from the bar, I slowly made my way over and sat down on one of the barstools.

"What brings you here?" Chance asked with a suspicious look on his face.

"I was just walking around and—"

"And…what? You just happened to stumble into a strip club," he said sarcastically while wiping down the bar.

"Kind of," I replied, smiling.

I turned in my chair to face the crowd, with my back to Chance.

"It's packed in here! Is it always this crowded? Why are there so many men with suits on?" I asked, sounding stupid and confused. I was also surprised to see how many women were in the crowd among the men.

"I see most of the same faces all of the time in here," Chance said before pointing to a group of men. "Those guys right there come in here every Tuesday and Friday, sometimes even Thursdays. Some of them come directly from work, which explains why they're all dressed up. Then you have the locals from the neighborhood that stumble in here every now and again. Then the women you see sometimes come in groups for a bachelorette party, after a wine tour, or simply to join their significant other."

"You'd think the women would want to see men, not other women," I said, perplexed.

"Well, unfortunately, there are no male strip clubs anywhere near here, so my guess is that they really don't have much of a choice. You'd be surprised at how into it these women can get. It's crazy to watch sometimes."

Then Chance looked at me, saw the look on my face, and apologized.

I swung my chair back around toward Chance and looked him dead in the eye, and as serious as I could, asked "How don't you have a hard-on the entire time these women dance?" I giggled like I was embarrassed that I said the words *hard-on*.

Then with a straight face, Chance looked at me and replied, "At first it was a bit difficult, but then I got to know each and every one of the girls—"

"You got to know each and every one of them, huh?" I teased, moving my eyebrows up and down.

"Lena, not like that! They're practically like family to me. I have no one here."

"Um, you have Bryan and me."

"Oh, I know that. This is just like a different type of family. Believe it or not, some of these girls are moms, some of them just do this to pay for college, a few of them just do it for fun, and some actually have day jobs and then come here afterward to make a little extra cash. Each of them has a story to tell. They're not just some stuck-up whores."

"Okay, let me cut you off there, buddy, I get it, they're like family," I said, smiling at him with my face propped up in my hands, elbows on the bar. "You're so darn cute, how do these women not throw themselves at you?" I asked jokingly.

"Weeeelllll," Chance said, dragging the word out.

"Hey," I said, throwing the cloth from the bar at him.

"I'm just kidding." He cracked up at the look on my face.

I swirled my chair back around toward the stage, and the next girl, who came out to Ginuwine's "My Pony," looked familiar, but I couldn't seem to place where I knew her from.

"I will be right back," Chance said as he walked from behind the bar toward a room off to the side of the bar.

I was mesmerized by this girl. She had my full attention. Her long, strawberry-blond hair flowed through the air, and every move she made up against that metal pole seemed like it was happening in slow motion mode. Then she slid all the way down with her back against the pole, until she let the pole go with her hands and placed them in front of her, and she suddenly was on all fours crawling around the stage. At one point she looked directly at me, we locked eyes, and she smiled, then continued with her show.

I began to get a warm fuzzy feeling, until Chance startled me.

CHAPTER 86

Lena

"I'm back," Chance said, slapping the bar, practically making me jump right out of my seat. "Oh, I'm sorry, I didn't mean to scare you. Wait a second! You were just totally checking Daisy out, weren't you!" Chance said, teasing me.

"No, I don't know what you're talking about!" I replied, embarrassed that I got caught. I could feel my cheeks turning red.

"It's okay. It's normal to feel that way about another girl. I see it all the time here. Daisy is great. She's a really, nice girl. Very easy to talk to."

"I'm sure she is really easy to talk to when she has her boobies all up in your face," I said, teasing Chance.

"Stop it," he said, laughing. "It truly isn't like that, I swear," but he couldn't stop laughing.

"Well, anyway, I came here to ask you if you'd like to be my plus-one at my best friend Becca's wedding next weekend. What do you think?"

"Yeah, absolutely! I'd love to go. Wait. What about Bryan? I thought he was going?" Chance asked, concerned.

"What about him? I changed my mind. He'll be fine. He's a grown-ass man. He can take care of himself while we're away," I snapped.

"Oh, no, I didn't mean to—"

"Gotcha!" I said. "I was just messing with you." I started laughing at his facial expression. "I couldn't help myself, I'm sorry. You

235

should've seen the look on your face," I said while hopping off the barstool. "I just changed my mind, that's all."

"Wait! Where are you going?" Chance wanted to know.

"I'm going to head home. I just wanted to swing in and ask you to be my date for the wedding."

"It's dark outside, though, and you shouldn't be walking alone. There's a serial killer running around here. You should be scared!"

"Yes, you're right, but I have my big-girl panties on. I'll be okay. See you later." I saluted toward Chance before pushing the door open with my butt.

I probably should be nervous walking home alone in the dark, but Silver Tree Acres is my hometown, where I was born and raised. It was hard for me to consider that it could be an unsafe place to live.

Right after thinking that, a chill ran up my spine. I suddenly felt like I was being watched. *It's just nerves,* I told myself. I shook off the thought and continued my walk home.

CHAPTER 87

Lena

While Chance and I were packing, gathering our last items together to get ready to leave for the airport, Bryan shocked us both by offering to drive us there, followed by a compliment, "Lena, you're going to look gorgeous in that bridesmaid gown."

Now any other day I would find this a sweet gesture and flattering compliment, but instead I was taken aback because of his reaction days before when I broke the news that I wanted to take Chance instead of him to the wedding. I felt like there was an underlying reason for this sudden change of heart.

Trying not to show my concern about his sudden change in behavior, I decided to go along with this charade as I rather him be like this rather than the terrifying blank stare mess he was the other night. "Oh, stop, you're making me blush."

As Chance and I were grabbing our luggage out of the back of the truck, Bryan yelled out, "Make sure you take pictures! Lots of them! Have fun you two! See you soon."

What I didn't catch onto at the time was his words of "See you soon." I guess that should've been the first hint, but I clearly missed it.

At the time that Chance and I were in the line to check our luggage, I noticed Jocelyn standing at the very front of the same line. She had a nice dress on and a scarf around her neck, which I thought was weird since it was like a thousand degrees outside, but I thought, *To each their own!*

Seeing Jocelyn gave me a huge sense of relief because when Bryan said she was dead, then paused, then said that he meant that she was dead to him. It had made me a little nervous. *Now I feel like such a jerk for even thinking he could do something like that. What a great friend I am.* Jocelyn never looked my way. *I couldn't help but wonder where she was going.*

Once we boarded the flight to Virginia and got situated in our seats, I couldn't contain my excitement thinking about Becca's wedding.

"I'm so darn excited," I said, tugging on Chance's sleeve, bouncing up and down in my seat as the plane was beginning to ascend into the air.

———

Becca had called me the night before to let me know that she wanted all her bridesmaids to spend the night at her place and she wanted the guys to spend the night at a hotel. So once our flight arrived at the Virginia airport, we collected our luggage, arranged an Uber, and made our first stop at the Hyatt to book a room for Chance.

When we walked into the hotel room, Chance walked straight toward the bed and flopped down face-first.

"We're supposed to meet up later with the group for dinner at Outback Steakhouse. Would you mind if I put myself together here, then we can just arrange for an Uber to take us to the restaurant about 5:30 p.m.?" I asked, already knowing what the answer would be I made my way toward the bathroom.

"Not at all. Have at it. Have a blast," Chance said, being sarcastic.

"I hope I'll do okay at the ceremony tomorrow since I couldn't be here today to practice with them," I said through the open bathroom door while applying my makeup.

"You'll do just fine," Chance reassured me while he flipped through the stations on the television.

"Don't you have to get ready?" I asked anxiously.

"I just have to throw on a nice shirt, which'll take all of five seconds."

Chance was buttoning up his shirt when I walked out of the bathroom with my bridesmaid's dress on. "Wow" was all that emerged from his mouth.

So I panicked of course from his reaction. "Oh my god, does the dress look bad? What's wrong?"

"Nothing's wrong. You look gorgeous. You clean up very well for being a farm girl."

"Ha-ha, very funny. I'm not quite sure if that was a compliment or not, but I'll take it." The dress was strapless, with an overlay of sparkling chiffon material and fit snug to my body.

When I looked down at the dress, I felt a little sad knowing that I bought the dress when Bryan and I went shopping together months earlier, and I'm pretty sure it was the same day we picked out Chewie. I remember his reaction was pretty much the same as Chance's when I walked out of the dressing room. He told me I was beautiful and shinier than the stars in the sky.

I stood there for a moment, feeling guilty for not bringing Bryan as my date.

"You okay?" Chance asked.

"Oh, yes, I'm fine," I said, snapping out of it, then going back to the bathroom to change for dinner.

CHAPTER 88

Lena

Dinner at the Outback Steakhouse went well. Chance got to meet everyone in the wedding party and some of their family and friends. They loved him. He fit right in.

When we all walked out of the restaurant, the girls went one way, the boys the other. I gave Chance a quick gentle kiss on the lips before we parted, and as I was getting into the Uber, I turned around to take one more look at him. I thought, *Wow, he would make a great husband and father.* Then, *Whoa, where'd that come from? Definitely the wine talking!*

After all the other girls went to bed, Becca and I stayed up just a little bit longer to catch up.

"Glass of wine?" Becca asked.

"Of course, my dear, why not."

"So you decided to bring the hunk with you instead of Bryan, huh?" Becca commented rather than asked.

"Yes, but it was a hard decision. I really care about both of them a lot. I truly think Bryan is my soul mate. Chance, well, he's definitely gorgeous, and he's really sweet, and I feel like he popped into my life for a reason, but…"

"Do you have any idea how fucked up that all sounds?" Becca asked rhetorically, and we both burst out laughing. "I bet Chance is reeeaaal sweet! Sweet with those girls at the strip club!" Becca gave me a stern yet not serious look, followed by a sly grin.

"No, he's not like that. Those girls are like his family," I said, calmly defending him.

Becca almost choked on her drink. "Did you hear what you just said?"

Becca must have noticed the stunned look on my face as she quickly followed up with, "I'm joking, I'm joking! Chance does seem like a really nice guy. I'm honestly glad you brought him rather than Bryan. There's something I never told you about Bryan," Becca said, long-faced.

"One day when I was walking home from school, I heard this strange squealing sound, followed by gurgling. Curious about what the noise was, I walked toward this shed where I heard the sound coming from. When I walked up and peeked around the corner, Bryan was standing there holding a limp cat in his hands." Becca took a big gulp of wine before saying, "Lena, I'm pretty positive that Bryan killed that cat."

"Becca!" I said giving her the "Are your serious right now?" look.

"Bryan would never hurt an animal, he loves them. He's one of the kindest people I know. He probably saw that it was hurt, picked it up, and it died just as you walked over there," I suggested, not even giving it a second thought.

"You know what, you're probably right, Lena," Becca said, trying to support her best friend. "I hope that you know that I'm just looking out for you."

I couldn't help myself from saying what I said next, "Yeah, you're really looking out for me all right, telling me that one guy I like is a whore and the other one is a killer." We both laughed so hard I almost peed my pants.

CHAPTER 89

Chance

Chance lay on the bed at the hotel room, with his right leg crossed over his left, hands behind his head, and just stared at the ceiling for a while, smiling. Shortly thereafter he decided to make a phone call.

"Hey, there, how's it going? Everything here has fallen into place perfectly. I finally made my decision, that I'm going to do it. I feel the timing is right, and I really think this is what Amanda would have wanted me to do. Tomorrow will be the perfect day!"

"Wish me luck" were his last words before hanging up.

CHAPTER 90

Lena

The next morning was a bit hectic, all the girls running around getting ready, putting their makeup on, getting their hair and nails done.

The ride in the limo was not very long. You could tell all the girls' nerves were on edge as not much chattering took place.

The ceremony at the church turned out to be absolutely beautiful but felt like it ended just as fast as it started. Becca looked stunning. I felt kind of sexy in my shiny purple dress and silver pumps, just like a sexy princess.

Once we wrapped up pictures at the church and Corona Park, the park Becca so desperately wanted her wedding pictures taken at, we made our way to the Kazperzack's reception hall. Once we arrived at the reception hall, we all had a little difficulty getting out of the limo as were all half-tanked from drinking so much wine during the limo ride.

While we were all standing in a room waiting to be announced as the wedding party, I swore I thought I saw Jocelyn pass by in the hall.

Most likely just a look-alike, I thought. *What would she be doing in Virginia? Then again, she technically could be in the same venue just at a different party, in one of the other rooms, since there was more than one reception happening. Why, for the love of God, am I even thinking about this right now!* I scolded myself. *It's time to have some fun!*

———

Then came the first shock of the night.

While we were eating dinner, Bryan suddenly walked through the door of the reception hall at Becca's wedding. He walked right over to the table where Chance was seated then sat in the empty chair next to him that was technically for me after we finished dinner.

I almost choked on my steak.

Becca leaned forward at the head table, looked down at me, and mouthed, "What the fuck?!"

I responded by raising my hands in the air as if to say, "I've no clue."

Once dinner was finished, I got up and walked over to the table where Chance and Bryan were seated.

"Bryan, what the hell are you doing here?" I sounded a bit harsh, more than I intended to.

Bryan looked directly into my eyes, and with a serious look on his face, he calmly said to me, "Lena, I should be the one here with you, not Chance." Then he turned and looked at Chance. "No offense to you, buddy."

As I stood there stunned, unsure what to say, Bryan continued, "Lena, I love you. I've loved you from the first time I laid my eyes on you. No other girl could ever in a million years take your place."

Then came the second shock of the night.

Bryan got down on one knee and opened a small black box that had the biggest, shiniest, heart-shaped diamond that I'd ever seen.

I couldn't move, like I was frozen in time. I was horrified. Embarrassed.

Finally, after what felt like forever, I blurted, "Oh my god, Bryan, get up! Please get up! Get up! I'm begging you."

"Does this mean your answer is no?" Bryan's voice cracked.

I could feel everyone's eyes on us. The music halted, and it became eerily quiet, and I could hear whispering all around us. It felt like I was trapped in a horrible nightmare. I was beyond livid that Bryan did this on my best friend's wedding day. *What the hell was he thinking?*

I looked over at Becca, who appeared pissed, which who could blame her, and I mouthed the words "I'm so sorry" to her.

Then came the third rude awakening of the night.

As I grabbed Bryan's arm to help get him up off the floor, I heard loud footsteps coming directly toward us. When I looked up to see who was approaching, it was three Virginia state police officers.

They walked right up to Chance, flashed their badges, and said, "Chance Wallace, you're under arrest for the murder of Amanda Keele in Cloverfield, Maine. You have the right to remain silent. Anything you say or do…" The officer's voices trailed off. I must have gone into shock as I no longer could hear anything except for my heart beating.

This must be a joke. I was absolutely in disbelief. All I could do was watch as they escorted Chance out of the room.

I felt hot, like I was going to be sick or pass out or maybe even both. As they were just about to exit the room, Chance yelled, "Lena, I didn't kill my fiancée! I should've told you about her. I'm so sorry! I'm not a killer, I promise! The truth will come out."

Then just like that Chance was gone.

Fiancée? Murder? I was so confused, embarrassed, and upset. *I'm going to wake up any second now. This is all just a really bad dream I kept telling myself.*

And just as I thought it couldn't possibly get any worse, the fourth and final bombshell hit. Three more Virginia state police officers walked into the reception hall, again coming in my direction. I thought to myself, *You have got to be fucking kidding me.* This time though, they handcuffed Bryan.

I looked on in horror.

"Bryan Wells, you're under arrest for the attempted murder of Jocelyn Greene and the murder of Gina Hedlidge. You have the right to remain silent…"

While they were escorting Bryan out of the reception hall, I caught sight of Jocelyn standing in the doorway.

Bryan struggled as the officers whisked him away, trying to look over his shoulder. "Lena, all of it was for you! Everything I did was for you! I love you. More than you'll ever know."

When the officers and Bryan were out of the way, I could clearly see Jocelyn, her scarf was removed, and I could see bruising in the shape of fingers, as if there had been hands around her neck.

Oh my god. Did Bryan really try and kill her? Did he really think she was dead? Is that what he meant when he said she was dead! Was he confessing to me?

I stood there, light-headed, for what felt like eternity but was only seconds. Watching the two men in my life get arrested one right after another at my best friend's wedding, it felt surreal.

The music came back on, and everyone went back to enjoying themselves like nothing had ever happened. I thought for sure Becca was going to come over and ask me to leave for ruining her wedding day, but oddly enough she didn't.

Then I felt a soft hand grab mine.

When I turned around to see who it was, there she stood, like a guardian angel. The strawberry-blond stripper, Daisy, from Wesley's was at my best friend's wedding, and then it hit me where I knew her from. We went to school together. Her real name is Gwen Shevon.

She ended up being my knight in shining armor. She came and saved me, the damsel in distress. Our eyes locked again, like they did when I was at the club. She was gorgeous and looked sexy as hell in a sparkly teal strapless dress.

She took my hand and walked me out onto the dance floor, where Becca was smiling at me. I felt relieved to know Becca didn't hate me after everything that had just taken place.

This definitely wasn't how I anticipated my night to end, especially at my best friend's wedding.

As the saying goes, everything happens for a reason!

Right?

About the Author

First-time writer, aspiring author, born and raised in Buffalo, New York. I am currently a banking officer at a local bank as well as a first time self-employed business owner of WillowHill Designs in Buffalo, New York. I live with my husband, Steve, and my two children, both boys. What started out as just jotting down words, thoughts, onto some loose-leaf paper while sitting next to my (late) mother, who was laying quietly in her bed at hospice, turned into a relaxing hobby, which then evolved into a book. I am currently working on my second book, which will be called *Bully*.

CPSIA information can be obtained
at www.ICGtesting.com
Printed in the USA
BVHW032148221020
591670BV00011B/35